ISLE OF
SWIMMING CATS

ISLE OF SWIMMING CATS

Another 'You Say Which Way' Adventure

Blair Polly & DM Potter

Published by:
The Fairytale Factory Ltd.
Wellington, New Zealand.
All rights reserved.
Copyright © 2019

ISBN:9781080665082

FAIRYTALE
FACTORY
YouSayWhichWay.com

How this book works

- This story depends on YOU.

- YOU say which way the story goes.

- What will YOU do?

At the end of each chapter, make a decision and then turn to the page that matches your choice. **P62** means turn to page 62.

There are many paths to try. You can read them all over time. Right now, it's time to start the story. Good luck!

Oh … and watch out for coconut crabs, they're hungry!

Table of Contents

ISLE OF SWIMMING CATS

The storm

As a chimpanzee settles into his leafy nest, he watches a mother cat wade out of the lagoon. Her kitten follows carrying a silver fish. Beneath his tree, the cats stop to eat.

A huge crab darts out of the undergrowth, claws snapping.

Hisssss! The mother cat whirls to face the threat, her sharp claws springing from paddle-sized paws ready to protect her young.

With a startled screech, the chimpanzee drops his coconut into the skirmish.

The crab scuttles back, giving the mother a second to grab her kitten by the scruff of its neck and bound away.

A large pincer clamps onto the abandoned fish and the crab drags it into the bushes.

Booms of thunder sound in the distance as a gust of wind sways the trees. Solid drops of rain begin to fall.

The chimpanzee pulls a leaf over his head, stares at his coconut lying on the ground and wonders if it's worth getting wet to retrieve it.

Beyond the reef, the storm rages.

"Get below!" the skipper yells, gripping the tiller with both hands and bracing his feet. A towering wave rises up behind the boat. "Now!"

Driving spray forces you to close your eyes as you clutch at handholds and duck through the hatch. Your watch is over. It's time to take a break from the howling gale.

The floor bucks as you strip off your wet weather gear and collapse into your bunk. A fun ocean cruise has turned into a survival story.

The stern of the yacht rises again. The cabin tilts at a steep angle.

With the lee cloth pulled up to stop you falling from your bunk, you listen to the water racing along the hull and the howl of the wind in the rigging above. You're in the middle of the South Pacific Ocean, miles from a safe harbor. It's not like you can get off, so you roll onto your side and try to put the drama out of your mind. You're so tired… can't keep… eyes… open.

You awake to a strange calm. The storm has passed, but your head is throbbing. There is a lump on your scalp. In the madness of your last watch, you must have banged into something.

You lower the lee cloth and swing your feet to the floor.

Splash!

Water in the cabin. That's not normal.

"Skipper?" You wade, ankle deep, down the companionway. "Hello?"

The captain's cabin is empty. So is the head. After checking the quarter berths for signs of life, you climb the steps from the main saloon, duck through the hatchway and emerge into the cockpit.

"Ahoy? Anyone here?"

Someone's lashed the tiller hard to port. At the bow, the yacht's smallest sail, a tiny storm jib, hangs in tatters. The storm lantern splutters, low on fuel.

The yacht is deserted.

Considering the strength of the storm, the sea is surprisingly calm. No whitecaps, just a slight swell rolling in from the northwest.

The tropical sun fries the back of your neck as you survey the tangle of ropes on deck.

How long have you been asleep? More importantly, where is everyone?

Apart from a small island in the distance, all you see is ocean.

Then you spot the empty brackets.

The life raft is gone!

A chill runs down your spine. Why would the rest of the crew leave without you? It makes no sense. They must have known you were asleep. Were you so tired you didn't hear the call to abandon ship? Have they gone to the island? But why use the life raft when they have the yacht?

Whatever the reason, you're here now. Alone. You'll just have to deal with it.

Maybe you should pump out the bilge. A yacht isn't much use if it's full of water. Or should you put out an emergency call on channel 16?

It's time for your first decision. Do you:

Pump out the bilges? **P5**

Or

Put out an emergency call on the radio? **P8**

Pump out the bilges

The handle for the bilge pump is in the cockpit. Quick up and down movements suck water from the bottom of the boat up through a plastic pipe and squirt it back into the ocean where it belongs.

After pumping for five minutes, you look below expecting to see the water level going down. But no. If anything, the water is deeper. And if more water is coming in than you can pump out, it only means one thing.

The boat is sinking.

You scan the horizon for help. Nothing. Your only hope is an island about three miles away.

Sailing to the island is out of the question. By the time you get the sails up the boat will be full of water. Instead, you start the diesel motor. As it warms up, you go forward, drop the shredded storm jib, tie it to the rail and coil up the ropes on deck so they don't trail overboard and get tangled in the propeller. Then you unlash the tiller and put the yacht into gear.

A quick peek below confirms that the water is still rising. It won't be long before it drowns the engine.

As you motor towards the island, you steer with one hand and pump like crazy with the other.

The weight of the water sloshing around in the hull doesn't help your speed. You aim the bow towards a gap in the island's protective reef, hoping to make it into the lagoon before the boat sinks.

The yacht get slower and slower as it sinks lower and lower. By the time you're through the reef, about a mile from shore, water is knee deep in the main saloon.

Splutterrrr… clunk!

The engine stops.

You run below and grab a lifejacket.

The yacht is dangerously low at the stern. Time to swim for it or you'll go down with the boat.

You tighten the straps on your lifejacket, rush up to the cockpit and step over the rail.

Splash!

"No sharks. Please, no sharks," you chant as you dogpaddle towards the beach.

By the time your feet touch the bottom of the lagoon, your arms ache.

You've never been so happy to feel sand in your life. As you slip off your life jacket, you turn just in time to see the yacht's mast slip beneath the surface.

You wring out your t-shirt and sit down to warm up in the sun.

Soon your clothes are dry, so you head off down the beach. Maybe your crewmates are nearby. After walking a hundred yards, you spot a track heading inland between two coconut palms and decide to go exploring.

The track is narrow and crowded by ferns and flowering plants. Mynah birds, dark in color with yellow flashes under their eyes, flit from branch to branch.

Bright green parrots squawk.

In the distance, a stony hill rises above the lush greenery. Maybe you'll spot where the crew landed or see signs of civilization from up there.

As you reach the outcrop's base, you realize what you're looking at is manmade and not a hill at all. Rectangular sections of stone interlock to form a dome about one hundred yards across and as high as a three-story building. It's as if someone's taken a huge bowl, turned it upside down, and pushed it into the ground. The sun-baked rock radiates heat. Spindly weeds wilt in the narrow gaps where the rectangular sections meet. Patches of bright yellow and pale green lichen create a scabby patchwork on its surface. The thing looks as ancient as the pyramids in Egypt.

So what now? Should you explore the structure further? Climb to the top and have a look around? Or should you get back to the beach in case the rest of the crew come looking for you or a boat turns up?

You need to make a decision. Do you:

Inspect the stone structure? **P12**

Or

Head back to the beach? **P14**

Put out emergency call on radio

"Mayday! Mayday! Mayday! This is yacht *Wanderlust*..."

Flash! Bang!

The stench of burning plastic fills your nose. Thick black smoke billows from the radio's control panel. Flames lick the wooden hull. You pull your tee shirt up over your mouth and click the radio transmitter one last time. "Mayday!"

Nothing. Not even static. So much for calling for help.

Where's the emergency locator beacon? At least if you set off the EPIRB authorities will know you're in trouble. But the EPIRB's not hanging in its normal spot. The crew must have taken it when they abandoned ship.

Can't stay down here. Smoke's filling the cabin.

Holding your breath, you snag a lifejacket and run for it.

The wind has come up. Waves are pushing the yacht towards the island, but the fire's taking hold. It's time to abandon ship.

You strap on the life jacket and leap over the rail.

Splash! At least here, in the tropics, the water isn't cold.

The island looks about a mile away. You should make it no problem, providing there aren't any hungry sharks around.

You spot a pair of palm trees on the beach and start kicking in that direction.

After fifteen minutes in the water, you're closer to shore, but a current is pulling you away from the beach and towards a rocky point where waves crash onto the reef.

You kick harder towards the safety of calm waters. But you're no match for nature. Exhausted, you flip onto your back and float, gasping for air.

Tons of water booms onto the rocks no more than a hundred yards away.

This is not good.

Just when you thought things couldn't get worse, a dark shape swims directly at you and brushes against your leg.

You kick out. "Get away from me!"

More dark shapes swarm around you. First two, then two more. Are they sharks attracted by your frantic kicking? Do they think you're a fish in distress?

If so, the jagged rocks are the least of your worries.

But the shapes look too small to be sharks.

When a cat's head pops out of the water in front of you, you nearly sob with relief.

"Meow!" the cat cries, its green eyes staring into yours.

What are cats doing out here in the water?

Three more cats surface. They all have the same short, grey fur, but as they paddle beside you, you notice their paws are larger than normal and their tails, although covered in hair, are long and shaped more like an eel's tail than a typical house cat's.

"Meow!" says another cat.

What is going on?

The waves crash on the rocks fifty yards away.

The four cats turn their backs to you and lift their tails out of the water right in front of your face.

"Meow! Meow!" the cats cry.

Are they trying to tell you something? Do they want you to grab their tails?

Breakers pound the rocks less than thirty yards away.

"MEOW!"

With nothing to lose, you grab two tails in one hand, and two in the other.

As soon as you have hold, the four cats start paddling. With four paws per cat, the animals have the power of a small outboard motor.

You lie flat on your stomach and kick your feet to help.

"It's working," you say to the cats, unsure if they understand.

"Meow," one says, looking back over its shoulder.

The cats are tireless. They paddle until you've rounded the point and are away from the dangerous waves before turning towards shore where thirty feet of near vertical rock rises from the water.

Squawking birds nest in holes high in the cliff.

"Where are you taking me?"

There is no answer from the cats.

Then you spot an entrance to a cave.

Set into the cliff, near the cave's opening, are the rungs of a rusty old ladder.

"Meow."

Are the cats taking you into the cave, or do they want you to let go and climb the ladder? It is time to make a decision. Do you:

Allow the cats to pull you into their cave? **P27**

Or

Leave the cats and climb the metal ladder? **P77**

YOU SAY WHICH WAY

Inspect the stone structure

The textured surface of the dome gives your sneakers plenty of grip, and sweat trickles down your forehead by the time you reach the top.

A circular capstone, about three steps across, covers the top of the dome. Carved into the capstone are the words:

AUTHORIZED PERSONNEL ONLY - ENTER AT OWN RISK

Enter? How could you enter even if you wanted to? There's no door. Have you missed something? You sit down and trace the words carved in the stone with your finger.

With a jolt, the capstone sinks an inch and begins to vibrate.

Yikes!

Before you have time to jump off, the capstone drops like a high-speed elevator.

"Going down," says a robotic voice. "Please keep hands clear of the walls."

"Whoaaa!" you shout, nearly losing your balance.

Grey walls whoosh by. Above your head, the circular patch of sky shrinks with every second. Moments later, the platform stops, and two doors open, revealing a small alcove with glistening white walls. On the far side of the alcove are two more doors.

"Please depart the elevator," the voice says.

"What if I don't want to get off?" you ask, crossing your arms and staying where you are.

Alarm bells ring. "Depart elevator now," the robotic voice says. "Depart elevator now!"

The voice gets louder with each repetition.

You clamp your hands over your ears. "All right, already. Don't get your circuits in a twist!"

Clunk, the doors close behind you.

So what now? There's no point in staying here. It's just an empty space. You take a few steps towards the two doors and read the words painted on their surface.

One says: AQUARIUM. The other says: LABORATORY.

It is time to make a decision. Do you:

Go through the door that says Aquarium? **P18**

Or

Go through the door that says Laboratory? **P80**

Head back to the beach

The path back through the jungle to the beach is alive with birdsong. A light breeze filled with the scent of flowers rustles the leaves in the trees above.

It's far more likely for the crew to stay near the water where they'll be visible to passing aircraft or boats. As you walk between the palm trees onto the beach, you spot a school of silvery fish leaping out of the water in the lagoon. Thinking a bigger fish must be after them, you sprint down to the water's edge to watch the show.

As a shower of fish fly into the air, a long-tailed cat leaps from the water, snapping and clawing in hot pursuit.

What?

Shaking your head, you blink a few times. "Huh?"

Are your eyes playing tricks? A cat? In the water?

The school of fish turns and heads for the opening in the reef, jumping and splashing as they go, but there's no further sign of whatever is chasing them.

"Must be seeing things," you mumble. "Sunstroke, maybe. Better get out of the heat for a while."

Is talking to yourself a sign of sunstroke?

You sit in the shade of a leafy bush and take stock of your situation. You didn't have time to take anything from the yacht apart from a hat you stuffed into your back pocket. You need to find water if you're going to last. You take off your shoes and plop the hat on your head.

"Time to walk around the island," you tell yourself. "The life raft and crew must be somewhere."

The sand is warm as it squishes up between your toes. In the distance, gulls fly over a rocky headland that protects the lagoon from the waves of the open ocean.

For a moment, the clear blue sky, swaying palm trees and clear water makes you feel like you're on vacation at a resort. Then when you remember the storm and the yacht sinking, the reality of your isolation comes crashing back.

Finding water and the rest of the crew have to be your first priorities. The life raft's radio and EPIRB, which sends out an emergency signal to passing aircraft and ships, are critical to your rescue.

Your eyes track left and right as you walk. About a quarter of a mile down the beach, a flash of orange catches your eye.

It's a life jacket from the boat. *Wanderlust* is written in black sharpie across its front. There were four crew and six life jackets on board when the yacht left Hawaii. You wore one life jacket when you abandoned ship and remember seeing another in the cabin before you left overboard. Including the one you've just found, that makes three, which leaves three for the other crew members. It could be worse.

You toss the life jacket up above the high tide mark and continue on towards the headland.

Further along, the beach narrows and the rocks begin. You stop and put your sneakers back on. Infections are common in the tropics, and every sailor knows coral cuts are bad news.

Thankfully, the tide is out, and with no waves to dodge, walking on the rocks isn't too difficult. Below a section of cliff, a flat rocky shelf juts out into the ocean. The shelf is potted with tidal pools and inhabited by hermit crabs, limpets, sea stars and tiny fish. Fat gulls dine at their favorite pool, while others use their beaks to winkle crabs from crevices in the rock. Further out, waves crash against the shelf, sending plumes of spray skyward.

Birds squawk loudly as you walk past, as if to say 'Keep away from my lunch!'

You're about halfway around the island when you spot the life raft jammed between two big rocks. It's partially deflated and tilted to one side.

"Ahoy!" you yell, running towards the raft. "Is anyone around?"

The only reply you get is a squawk from a hungry gull.

The raft is empty. No radio. No EPIRB. No crew members. Nothing but half a bottle of water which you gulp down.

Refreshed, you try to pull the raft out from between the rocks, but it's wedged tight.

This spot would be treacherous at high tide. You can imagine the scene as the raft came ashore—you picture it rising up as the water shallows along the flat shelf of rock before being tossed against the jumble of rocks at the bottom of the cliff.

It would be difficult to survive coming ashore here in stormy conditions, especially at night.

"Ahoy!" you yell up the cliff, in the hope someone managed to scramble up. "Is anyone there?"

Silence.

Sadness overcomes you as you think about the crew. It's not as if you've known them for long, but a few weeks sailing together can forge strong bonds. Or at least that's what you thought. But how strong could that bond be if the skipper and other two crew members abandoned ship without you? Maybe you didn't know them at all.

You run your fingers through your hair as you try to think.

So what now? Should you climb the cliff and see if the crew somehow made it to the top? It looks pretty steep. Or should you keep going around the island and see what else you might find?

It's time to make a decision. Do you:

Climb up the cliff and look for the crew? **P98**

Or

Keep walking around the island? **P22**

Go to the aquarium

The door swings back, and you enter a large room filled with shimmering blue light. The far wall is made of glass—an aquarium full of sea creatures.

Along the wall to your left, a clutter of equipment is arranged neatly along a stainless-steel bench. Another large tank, twice your height and filled with water, sits in the middle of the room. To your right is a round door with a sign above it that says AIRLOCK.

Your sneakers squeak on the glistening white floor as you walk up to the glass wall.

Schools of fish dart left then right with larger fish close behind. A huge manta ray glides past, its wings moving up and down gracefully as it flies through the water. Bright orange starfish and anemones of various colors sit amongst the colorful corals. Crabs scuttle back and forth in search of food.

In the distance you see a sad but familiar sight. Your yacht, lying on its side, wedged into the reef. This isn't a big aquarium. It's the lagoon.

You tap the glass, wondering who built such a place.

A red and white fish swims up to you and shakes its head as if telling you off.

"Seriously? I'm getting told not to tap on the glass by a fish?"

As you watch the scene in the lagoon, you think about your predicament. At least you haven't washed up on a deserted island. With all this equipment around, there must be people here too. Maybe you should have tried the lab door instead.

Pssssstttttt.

With a rush of air, the airlock door opens, and a girl with a shock of curly hair drips her way into the room. She's wearing a swimsuit and is drying herself with a dark blue towel. At first, she doesn't notice you.

"Ah hum…" you say, clearing your throat.

The girl's eyes widen as her head snaps around. "Crikey! Wha—what are you doing here?"

You smile and try to look as non-threatening as possible. "I was about to ask you the same question. What is this place?"

Seeing your smile, she relaxes a little. "I live here. My parents are scientists."

"But what's with the dome and the elevator? Seems a strange place to live."

She shrugs. "Place used to be a nuclear missile silo run by the American military. It closed down thirty years ago. A few years back, my parents moved here to do research. They'd had enough of Sydney and wanted to get away from Australia for a while."

"So where are your parents now?"

"On a supply run. It's just me at the mo."

"What? They've left you here alone?"

She finishes with the towel and hangs it on a rail by the door. "I'm fourteen, I can look after m'self."

"I hope they didn't get hit by the storm."

"They're fine. They took *Gerty* to Majuro first thing this morning after the storm blew through."

"Gerty?"

"Our float plane."

"Oh. You've got one of those?"

"Yep. She's a ripper."

You're not sure what she means by 'ripper', but she's smiling so it must be good.

"Majuro's in the Marshall Islands, isn't it?"

"Yep," she says before pulling on a long t-shirt she's taken off a hook by the door.

"How often do they go there?" you wonder. Maybe you can catch a lift next trip.

"Twice a year," she says.

Your heart sinks. "Twice a year? That's it?"

This is not looking good. You turn and look through the glass into the lagoon. "Our yacht sank," you say, pointing towards *Wanderlust*. "How am I supposed to get home?"

The girl shrugs. "Dunno." She turns and peers through the glass. "Where's the rest of your crew?"

"I was looking for them when I climbed up the dome. You didn't see a life raft or anyone else when you were out swimming, by any chance?"

She shakes her head. But there is something in her face that makes you wonder if she's telling the truth.

"I'm Wanda, by the way," the girl says. "What's your

name?"

Not sure if you want her to know your real name yet, you pause a moment. When a funny-looking shellfish swims past the window, you get an idea. "My friends call me Shrimp."

"Shrimp. Hmmm… So tell me, Shrimp. Do you like cats?"

"Yeah, sure. Who doesn't like cats?"

"Cool. Follow me."

Wanda walks towards the door marked AIRLOCK and pulls it open.

What do you do? Do you:

Go into the airlock? **P37**

Or

Make an excuse not to go into the airlock? **P68**

Keep walking around the island

The cliff looks too dangerous to climb, so you decide to keep going. It's tricky picking your way among the rocks. Many are slimy from spending half their time under the tide, but it's better than risking a fall down the cliff.

Occasionally you stop and peer into tidal pools where tiny fish, crabs, starfish and limpets and other sea creatures make their home. Gulls peer into some of the pools in search of food. They squawk at you as you pass.

After a mile or so, the rocks give way to a narrow shingle beach. Waves rush in, tumbling the stones like a cement mixer before rushing back out.

It's not until you get around the next headland that you spot a secluded cove sheltered between two rocky points. But it's not so much the cove that's interesting, it's the ship anchored in it. You recognize it at once!

It's the *Tex-plorer*, a large ice-strengthened research vessel, fitted out for ocean voyages anywhere on the globe. You've watched the *Tex-plorer* TV program ever since you were knee-high to a grasshopper. Tex, the host of the show, takes a camera crew to isolated locations around the world and teaches the TV audience about the wildlife they encounter.

An inflatable dingy sits on the sand above the high-tide mark.

There's no sign of any people.

"Ahoy!" you yell at the top of your voice. "Is anyone

here?"

"Cut!" It's the voice of a man. "Who's a'making all that racket? We're trying to work here." A sour-faced Tex emerges from the jungle, a giant coconut crab grasped firmly in one hand, a glistening machete in the other, followed by his camera operator. "Who in God's name are you?"

"Sorry. I–I didn't mean to interrupt your shoot," you say, staring up at your childhood hero.

Tex is dressed exactly as you've seen him on TV numerous times. Grey cargo shorts, sturdy boots, and an old army shirt with a Texan flag sewn above one of the pockets. On his head is his trademark white Stetson.

You kick the sand and feel your face redden. "I'm shipwrecked. I don't suppose you've seen the rest of my crew?"

"Well, as it happens, I have."

The day is getting better. "Really? Where?"

Tex raises a gnarled hand and points towards his ship. "Found 'em floating just off the coast as we came in. They'd abandoned their life raft before it hit the rocks and made a swim for it."

"So they're aboard your ship?"

Tex nods. "And mighty lucky they are to be there. Now if you can keep from jabbering for a few minutes, we'll just finish shooting this sequence on coconut crabs and then we can go back to the ship."

Without another word, Tex and the camera operator

turn and tromp back into the jungle.

You exhale a long sigh of relief and walk toward the inflatable. Tex sure is a lot grumpier in person than he is on TV.

While Tex finishes shooting the scene, you poke around the beach, checking out the shells and stones. One of the stones you find is clear and red. A garnet, perhaps. You pop it into your pocket just as Tex emerges from the jungle.

"Giddy-up, partner," he yells over at you. "Let's getta move on. I'm so hungry I could eat the south end of a north-bound longhorn."

Pleased to be leaving the island, you look forward to seeing your crew again. You give Tex and the camera operator a hand dragging the inflatable down the beach, and climb in while Tex starts the small outboard, shattering the solitude.

When you reach the *Tex-plorer,* the rest of your crew is waiting beside the rail to welcome you aboard. You head down to the saloon, where the boat's cook rustles up some Texas-sized steaks and fries. As you eat, the yacht's skipper tells you how he'd yelled out to abandon ship before being washed overboard and blown away from the yacht by the gale-force winds.

"We were lucky Tex arrived when he did. We'd been in the water all night and most of the morning. Had to abandon the raft 'cause it was going to hit the rocks."

After Tex eats his steak, he stands up. "I'm going to

tell the captain to get underway. We've got a couple more stops in the Marshall Islands before we head home to Hawaii. Why don't y'all go get some sleep? We've got at least 12 hours steaming before we get to Maduro."

Your crew agrees and heads down below to their cabins, while Tex climbs the steps to the bridge to help the captain set course for their next stop two hundred miles away.

You're about to go below for a much-needed sleep when you feel the vibration of the ship's engine through the floor and decide to take one last look at the island before departure.

You exit the cabin, walk down the port side of the ship to the stern, and look over the rail. It's then that you see a cat-like shape in the water. You lean out over the rail to get a better look, just as the ship exits the sheltered cove and smacks into a large wave. Before you know it, you're tipped up and flung over the side.

Splash!

You surface with a splutter. "Help!" you yell. "Kid overboard!"

But nobody hears your call. The ship increases speed, turns to starboard and disappears behind the headland.

"You've got to be kidding me…" you mutter as you start to swim back to shore. "Again?"

When you reach the beach, you sit in the sand and wonder how long it will take for you to get rescued this time. The crew of the *Tex-plorer* won't miss you for at least eight hours. They'll think you're fast asleep in your cabin. Once they do realize you're gone, they'll have no idea when you went over the side.

As you sit on the beach contemplating your fate, a large cat emerges from the water and pads up to you. Its fur is sleek, its paws large and its tail much longer than a normal cat's.

You've heard rumors of these aquatic cats, but always thought they were just stories sailors told to pass the time.

The cat pads up to you. "Meow!"

You give it a scratch. "Hello, puss, was that you I saw in the water?"

The cat rubs against you. "Meow."

Oh well, you might be shipwrecked again, but at least you have company this time.

This part of your story is over. But that's okay because there are many more story lines you can take. Have you come across the chimpanzees yet, or found the moon pool? Or you could start the story over again and make different choices. Who knows where you might end up?

Time to make a decision. Do you:

Go back to the beginning? **P127**

Or

Go to the Big List of Choices? **P125**

Let the cats take you into the cave

It's dark in here, but still the cats keep swimming deeper and deeper into the cave. You rise and fall as the ocean swell enters and exits the cave.

"Where are you taking me?" you ask the cats, not really expecting a response.

The cats swim on.

Then you spot a glow under the water in front of you. Where is the light coming from? It can't be natural. It's coming from under the water.

As the cats swim towards the light, you can begin to make out the walls of the cave. They are circular and smooth, like they've been cut by a huge drill.

The light gets brighter. It's about six feet down and coming from a circular hole cut in the rock. You can even read a sign attached to the rock wall over the hole. It says: MOON POOL ENTRY.

One of the cats turns towards you. "Meow!" it says before angling down and swimming towards the hole.

Clutching tighter to the cats' tails, you suck in a deep breath before your head goes under and kick hard as the cats power towards the light. Once through the hole you pop up on the other side.

You're in a circular pool inside a chamber with a domed roof. Thousands of LEDs make the roof look like the night sky. Beyond the pool is a flat area of concrete and a door with a control panel next to it. Above the door is a sign that says AIRLOCK. An ice chest sits against the wall.

You let go of the cats' tails, dogpaddle to the edge of the pool and pull yourself out.

"What is this place?"

One of the cats climbs out of the pool, walks over to the ice chest, and rubs its face against the side. "Meow."

You know that call. The cat wants whatever is in the chest.

"You hungry, are you?"

"Meow."

You drip your way over and unlatch the lid. The cooler is full of silver fish.

"Meow!" the cat says more insistently.

Another cat rubs its wet fur against your leg. "Meow!"

"Well, I suppose a few fish is fair payment for rescuing me." You toss one to each of the four cats and close the lid. "There you go."

As the cats eat, you study them. They're not that different from regular house cats. Just bigger and with much larger paws. But it's their tails that are the strangest. You noticed them when they were towing you towards the cave. About half again as long as a normal house cat, powerful and a bit flat like an eel's. You imagine how fast the cats could swim if they didn't have to tow you behind.

One by one, the cats finish eating their fish, pad back to the pool and dive in. Before you know it, you're alone again.

You shake your head. What a strange place.

The control panel by the airlock door has two lights. One red and the other green. The green one is shining. The door has a circular handle that spins around to open, like the ones you've seen in movies about submarines.

Green means go, doesn't it?

You turn the handle.

Pssssstttttt. Air rushes out as the door opens.

You step into a small cubical with another door on the far side. You know that with airlocks only one door can be open at a time, so you close the door before opening the next one.

This next room is much bigger. One wall is solid glass that looks out into the lagoon like a giant aquarium; another is lined with a stainless-steel bench covered with scientific equipment.

In the center of the room sits a huge glass tank full of water. Inside the tank an octopus with a rusty brown body, long tentacles and large black eyes stares at you.

The eyes follow you around the room.

"Holy moly," you say, inspecting the animal from near the glass. "Aren't you a big one?"

You're so busy staring at the octopus, you don't notice a tentacle slip over the top of the tank and slither down the glass towards your head.

"Bad Oscar! Get back in your tank!"

You glance up, following the gaze of the girl who's just entered the room, and see a tentacle with suckers the size of quarters dangling inches above you.

"Oscar! In your tank. Now!"

The tentacle slides up the glass, flips over the rim and plops back into the water.

"Lucky I came in when I did," the girl says. "Oscar was about to get friendly."

"How friendly?"

She smiles. "Let's just say he likes hugs."

"Tha–that thing is a pet?"

"A patient, really. My parents are nursing him back to health."

"He's sick?"

"Injured. Was nearly dead when my parents found him floating in the lagoon."

"What happened?"

The girl shrugs. "An orca, we think. Almost lost one of his tentacles. Luckily for him, Dad managed to stitch it back on. He's due for release soon."

The girl walks to a water cooler and pours you a drink.

You take the water gratefully and knock it back in one go. "Ahh… good," you say, wiping your mouth with your arm before looking back at the girl. "So your parents are doctors?"

"Biologists. They study what makes life tick. On the island here, that's cats, mainly."

"The ones with the long tails?"

The girl raises an eyebrow. "You've seen them?"

"My boat sank. I had to swim to the island but got caught in a rip. The cats saved me from getting tossed on the rocks and led me into a cave and through an underwater tunnel." You glance towards the airlock door.

She follows your gaze. "Oh… to the moon pool?"

"Is that what you call it?"

"And I bet you gave them fish as a reward."

Your eyes widen. "How did you know?"

A peal of laugher fills the room. "Those cats! They are so bad. They'll do anything for a meal."

"You mean they saved me just to get food?"

"Not entirely." She chuckles again. "But yeah. Believe me, you're not the first person they've tricked."

In any case, who are you to complain? If a cat wants some fish for saving your life, fish they will get, every time.

Then she giggles again, but in a friendly way. Not laughing to make you feel bad.

"So what's your name?" you ask the girl.

"Wanda."

"Where are your folks?"

"They've taken the floatplane to get supplies."

"They left you here alone?"

"I can take care of myself," she says.

"How long are they away?"

"Three days."

You'll be getting no help from them then.

"I don't suppose you've seen the rest of my crew?"

Wanda shakes her head. "No, but I've got an idea how we can find them."

"Really?"

She nods. "We promise the cats fish if they help."

This is confusing. "But how will they know what we want them to do?"

"We tell their leader."

"The cats have a leader?"

"Too right they do. Lots of animals have a pecking order, ya know, not just chickens."

You scratch the back of your head, and think. "But how do you tell the leader what you want?"

"Follow me. I'll show you."

Wanda leads you out of the room into a lobby and up an elevator. When the lift stops, you're standing on top of a stone dome with a view over the island.

"From up here, I can call the cats."

You look at the strange structure beneath your feet. "But what is this place?"

"It used to be a secret army base. Now it's my parents' laboratory."

Before you have a chance to ask another of the many questions racing through your head, Wanda reaches into her pocket and pulls out an oval piece of wood slightly longer than her hand. It has a braided cord tied to a hole in one end.

"What's that?" you ask.

"A bullroarer."

Wanda holds the string and lets the wooden part dangle. Then by swinging the bullroarer around her head, faster and faster, it makes a roaring sound. As it speeds up, it's almost as loud as a revving motorcycle. The faster she swings the bullroarer, the higher the pitch and the louder the sound.

Vroom, vroom, vroom, vroom. Vroom, vroom, vroom, vroom, hums the bullroarer as it whips around in a circle.

Abruptly, she stops, wraps up the cord, puts the bullroarer back in her pocket and sits down on the warm sunbaked stone. "Now we wait."

"For cats?"

She nods. "Yup."

You shrug and sit down beside her. "I've never called a cat like that. Puss, puss, puss, usually works for me."

Wanda smiles. "You'll see."

And you do. As if by magic, cats creep out of the jungle and climb up the slope of the dome towards where you and Wanda are sitting.

"Which is the leader?" you ask.

"You'll know him when you see him," Wanda says with a sparkle in her eye. "He's kinda different from the others."

"What's the leader's name?"

"We call him Kong."

"Because he's king of the cats?"

Wanda nods. "You got it."

Most of the cats are a little larger than the average house cat, but when a huge charcoal-colored cat comes striding out of the jungle and climbs the dome, there is no doubt in your mind that this is Kong.

"Wow," you exclaim. "He's the size of a cheetah!"

"Not wrong there, matey," Wanda says. "Nobody messes with Kong."

But then a strange thing happens. Kong ignores you. Instead, he climbs awkwardly into Wanda's lap and rubs his face against hers. His purr is nearly as loud as the bullroarer.

She grunts under his weight, but scratches him under the chin and rubs the soft fur of his belly. The other cats rub against you, wanting some cuddles too. So many cats!

After a while, Wanda pushes Kong away and turns to you. "Have you got something from the boat Kong can sniff?"

"Just me," you reply. "I didn't have time."

"Okay, well, let Kong get a whiff of yer hand then."

You move your hand towards Kong's face.

Kong licks your hand with a sandpapery tongue that nearly takes off the top layer of skin.

"Kong," Wanda says, regaining the animal's attention. "Listen to me, Kong. Go find the other people and you can have fish."

"Meow?" Kong says.

"Fish," Wanda says.

"Meow, meow?"

"Fish, fish," Wanda replies.

"What are you doing?" you ask. "Does he actually understand you?"

"He knows the word fish, that's for sure. And when I promise him fish, he always seems to work out what I want him to do. He's clever like that."

You tilt your head sideways and squint. To say you're skeptical is an understatement, but before you have a chance to ask more questions, Kong turns to the other cats and makes a series of mews and meows. They stop rubbing against you and take careful notice of their leader.

Then with a final hiss, Kong dispatches the cats into the jungle. Kong takes one last look at you, turns his back and saunters down the dome as if he's king of the world.

You glance over at Wanda. "Was that Kong issuing orders?"

Wanda nods.

"So what now?" you ask.

"We wait."

"Just wait?"

"Yup. If your friends are on the island, the cats will find them."

You're not sure if Wanda is playing a joke on you or if she really believes she has the ability to communicate with Kong. Maybe Wanda's been the only kid on the island for too long and is living in a fantasy world. If so, you could be waiting here for a long time. Maybe you should go and look for the crew yourself.

It's time to think. Wanda did get on with Kong pretty well. But what cat doesn't like a good scratch? That's not evidence of communication on anything but a very basic level. But then what if she's right? Maybe the cats are searching right now. Will they find the crew?

It's time to make a decision. Do you:

Wait with Wanda for the cats to find the crew? **P85**

Or

Go look for the crew yourself? **P92**

Go into the airlock

After stepping through the door, Wanda closes it and screws it tight with a round handle. A control box with buttons and a pressure dial is bolted to the wall.

Wanda turns a dial and pushes a green button. "This outer door is airtight so when we open the inner door, the air pressure will keep the water from rising up and flooding the chamber.

"I'll just get the pressure up a little and then we can check out the moon pool."

"Moon pool?"

"Probably easier to show you than explain," Wanda says, turning her attention back to the gauge.

The dial slowly rises from 14.7 pounds up to 15.0 pounds per square inch.

"Right, positive pressure," she says, pushing the red button and reaching for the handle of the inner door. "Check this out."

Psssstttttt.

On the other side of the door is a circular pool about twenty feet across. The roof is a dome with LEDs sparkling like stars.

"Wow!" Your eyes dart around the chamber. "This is awesome."

"You haven't seen anything yet." Wanda walks to the edge of the pool, kneels down and runs a finger along the surface of the water.

The little ripples created by her finger make the reflected light in the pool's surface dance back and forth as if the whole pool is alive.

"Here, puss, puss, puss," she sings.

You kneel down beside her. "What are you doing? Calling catfish?"

She glances up and nods towards a plastic box sitting against the wall. "Go get some fish from that cooler over there and I'll show you."

Curious to discover what she has in mind, you wander over and open the lid. "How many do you want?"

"Four should do it. Put them on the ground by the edge of the pool."

You do as Wanda asks.

While continuing to run the fingertips of one hand back and forth across the surface of the water, she grabs a fish with the other and holds it under the surface of the water. "The scent of this should do the trick."

It isn't long before you notice movement in the pool. Dark shapes, swimming around in circles, rising towards the surface with each rotation. There are three—no, four of them.

"Come here, puss, puss, puss," Wanda croons.

You gasp when a cat breaks the surface and glides towards Wanda using sweeps of its long tail for propulsion. "You really were calling cats! I thought you were joking."

With one hand, Wanda scoops up the animal and

holds the fish up to its nose. "Want some fish, kitty?"

"Meow!" the cat says before chomping into the fish.

Wanda strokes the cat's smooth grey coat. "Pretty kitty."

As she pets the animal, you give it a quick once over. This is no normal cat, that's for sure.

"Why are its paws so big and tail so long?"

"It evolved that way."

"But how?" you ask.

Wanda is about to answer when three more cats climb out of the pool and chomp into the other fish. As they eat, they stare at you suspiciously, as if you're about to steal their meal.

"Nice kitties," Wanda says in a soft voice. "Don't worry, Shrimp's a friend."

"Yeah. Nice kitties. Besides, I'm not a fan of raw fish."

Wanda puts the cat she's been holding down beside the others and stands up. "My parents are scientists. They've been breeding these cats to solve the aquatic rat problem."

"Huh? Aquatic rats?"

Wanda tries to keep a straight face, but she's a terrible liar and snorts. "No, I'm kidding. Aquatic rats? Really? You believed that?"

"If there are aquatic cats, why not rats? I've heard of aquatic iguanas living in the Galapagos Islands."

Wanda nods. "Yes, iguanas, that's right. These cats have evolved like the Galapagos iguanas did, except over a much shorter period. When the American military were here operating the missile silo, they must have had a few cats as pets. When they closed the base, the military left the cats behind. When the cats ran short of things to eat on land, they had no option but to hunt fish in the lagoon." She nods at the cats devouring the fish.

"So…?"

"So my parents heard accounts of swimming cats from a sailor they met in Sydney and decided to come and study them."

"But how did they grow such long tails?" you ask.

"We suspect it's a mutation caused by leaking radiation," Wanda replies. "They think the best fisher-cats had long tails, so they were the most successful breeders. They still spend a lot of their time on land. They just go into the water when they're hungry."

You look into Wanda's eyes. Is she pulling your leg again? You're not sure if you should believe her story or not. "Mutants?"

She spots your disbelief. "No, really. In such a small and isolated population of cats, it would only take one dominant individual to parent a whole clowder of long-tailed cats."

"A clowder?" you ask. "What's that?"

"It's what experts call a group of housecats. Personally, I think they should change the name to a chowder of cats, 'cause these guys really love fish. Did you know a group of cats can also be called a clutter or a glaring?"

"The way that those cats are glaring at me, that sounds about right."

Wanda chuckles. "Don't worry, they don't bite." She pauses a moment. "Unless I ask them to."

When Wanda sees your eyes widen in alarm, she laughs. "Chill. I'm joking!"

But is she?

Once the cats finish their meals, they slip back into the pool and swim off.

"There's an opening in the moon pool that leads back to the sea," Wanda says. "Watching the cats eat has made me hungry."

You missed breakfast, so your stomach is rumbling too. You're also really, really thirsty.

Wanda nods towards the airlock. "Shall we go have some peanut butter and jelly sandwiches?"

Do you trust food that is given to you by a stranger? After all, you don't know her very well. You could always make an excuse. Or do you trust her until you have a reason not to? Besides, if she is eating the food too…

What do you do? Do You:

Go have a peanut butter and jelly sandwich? **P42**

Or

Make an excuse not to have a sandwich? **P68**

Peanut butter and jelly sandwiches

Wanda takes you back through the airlock, out through the aquarium room and into the lobby. "Lift up," she says.

The lift doors open and the two of you pile in. Soon, you and Wanda are standing on top of the dome. Most of the island is visible from up here.

"Our house is this way," Wanda says.

You follow her down the dome, into the jungle and along a path that leads in the opposite direction as the lagoon.

The trees get larger as you trek deeper into the jungle. Many are covered in a tangle of hanging vines. Bright blue butterflies, green and black dragonflies, and an assortment of smaller insects flit through the undergrowth.

Off in the distance you hear a strange hooting sound. "What's that?"

"Chimpanzees," Wanda answers. "There are about fifty on the island. I'll introduce you later if you like."

A smile crosses your face. "Sounds almost as good as eating a peanut butter and jelly sandwich."

After walking for a few more minutes, a wooden structure appears high in the trees. A narrow ramp made from branches and vines spirals around a massive tree trunk up into the canopy.

"You live in a tree house?"

Wanda smiles. "Pretty awesome, eh?"

As you climb the ramp, you're thinking awesome is an understatement. The house is made of rough sawn planks, bamboo poles and vines. It spans two massive trees. Swing bridges and ramps link various rooms and levels.

The first room contains four cane armchairs, a table, stools and a kitchen bench made from hardwood boards. Cupboards and an old-fashioned refrigerator fill the wall behind the bench. The other walls are only three feet high, their top half open to the tropical breeze.

Wanda sets out bread and a jar of peanut butter. From the fridge, she removes a jar and holds it up for inspection. "Papaya jam," she says. "Homemade."

Wanda points you to a big water cooler and starts slapping together two sandwiches. Once you've quenched your thirst, you watch hungrily as she prepares the food.

But when she's finished, rather than moving to the table, Wanda puts the food in a satchel and walks over to a narrow staircase that zigzags up into the branches. "Let's eat in the crow's nest. We can see the whole island from up there. Maybe we'll spot your crew."

Some stairs and a swing bridge take you up a level where you come to a narrow ladder. The ladder creaks and sways a little as the two of you climb higher and higher into the canopy. Holding tightly onto the handrail, you try not to look down. Soon you reach a small platform and sit down on a large cushion.

"You really can see the whole island," you say. "How high are we?"

"Sixty feet, I reckon," Wanda says. "These are the tallest trees on the island."

You do some mental division. Sixty feet divided by twelve feet per floor. "As high as a five-story building, then."

Wanda considers what you've said and nods. "I suppose. I've never been in a building this high."

You demolish your sandwich and then study the landscape. From this vantage point, you can see over the canopy all the way to the ocean beyond. In some spots, you can see the beach. The passage through the reef to the lagoon is much more obvious from this height and the water looks so clear, it's almost like there's none at all. Bright corals make the lagoon look like an abstract painting.

Then you spot a single mast rising beyond the greenery of the jungle.

"Whose boat is that?" you ask, pointing. "I can't see the hull. Trees are blocking my view."

Wanda leaps to her feet and stares into the distance. "They're anchored on the northern end of the lagoon. I hope they're not catnappers."

The image of a bunch of sailors asleep on a couch pops into your head. "Catnappers? Is that a thing?"

But Wanda is serious. "An aquatic cat would be worth

a fortune to the right collector. My parents hoped our isolation would keep them safe. Very few people even know this island exists."

"Well, someone's let the cat out of the bag," you say with a smirk.

Wanda ignores your joke and starts down the steps. "Quick, we need to get to the lagoon."

Wanda is far quicker down to the ground than you are, but you catch up on the path back to the dome.

As you jog past the dome, you shout at Wanda's back. "So what are we going to do?"

She slows for a moment and glances over her shoulder. "Find out what they're up to."

"And if they're after the cats?"

"Then we've got a problem."

Not far from the beach, Wanda slows her pace, steps off the path and uses the shrubs and ferns as cover. "Stay low. We don't want them to see us."

For the last few yards, the two of you wriggle like snakes to the edge of the jungle and peek through the shrubbery.

The yacht is a hundred yards away, bobbing at anchor. Three men in tattered shorts and t-shirts are lowering an inflatable boat into the water.

Wanda whispers, "Looks like they're coming ashore. We'd better get back to the dome and disable the lift. We don't want them stumbling across the lab."

The two of you jog back along the path. Wanda's like a

mountain goat as she scurries to the top of the dome. You're rushing to keep up. Once on the capstone, the lift takes you down to the small white lobby.

"Lock lift," Wanda commands.

There's a swooshing sound and a short time later, a mechanical click. A red light flashes on above the lift door. "Now the men can't come down if they climb on top."

You're impressed with the technology in this place. But your mind is on the men in the boat. "But how are we supposed to watch them from down here?"

"We won't. We'll go out through the moon pool. Once we're in the bay, there's a ladder up to the top of the cliff. From there we'll be able to keep an eye on their boat."

"Sounds like a plan."

"Wait here," Wanda says. "I need to grab a couple of things from the lab."

While you wait, you worry about the men on the yacht. What if they are catnappers? What if they're armed and dangerous? They had the look of ex-military. You two are just teenagers. What can you do to stop them?

Wanda reappears with a waterproof flashlight and a pair of binoculars in her hand. "Righto, let's go."

In the aquarium room an octopus stares at you through the glass of the large tank.

"I didn't see that octopus last time I was here," you tell Wanda.

"Oh, that's Oscar. He's great at hiding."

You wave. "Hi, Oscar."

The tip of a tentacle wriggles.

"Did he just wave back at me? I've heard that octopuses are intelligent, but they don't understand English, do they?"

"Octopi are cephalopods like squid and cuttlefish. They're smart that's for sure. Just how clever, scientists are still finding out. Oscar will follow basic commands in exchange for food, so I reckon he's as smart as a dog. He's been very friendly since my parents rescued him."

"Wow. They don't look very smart."

"Looks can be deceiving. It took him less than an hour to figure out how to unlock the lid of his tank, so we don't even bother with it these days. Which reminds me, we'd better release him back into the ocean now that his injury has healed. I hate for him to be stuck if something happened to us."

"How do we do that?"

Wanda grabs a large plastic tub from the side of the room and slides it over towards Oscar's tank. "I'll just get him some shrimp."

From another smaller tank, Wanda nets a big load of live shrimp and dumps them in the tub.

"Come on, Oscar. Chow time."

There is no need to ask Oscar twice. He swims up to the top of his tank, slips over the edge and slides down into the plastic tub, where he starts eating the shrimp.

"Looks like he's done this before," you say.

"A few times," Wanda says, nodding. "Right, help me slide him into the airlock."

As you help Wanda maneuver Oscar and the tub through the airlock, she tells you how her parents saved Oscar after he was attacked by an orca and nearly killed.

You imagine having a pet octopus you could train. Sit, Oscar. Squirt ink, Oscar. Shake tentacles, Oscar.

Once through the airlock, you and Wanda enter a room with a glistening pool at its center. LED lights sparkle on the ceiling like stars in the night.

"This is the moon pool. It leads to the open ocean," Wanda says.

The two of you pull the tub near the edge of the water.

"Once Oscar's eaten the shrimp, he'll be able to get into the water and go back to the ocean."

Wanda sits on the edge of the pool and turns on the flashlight. She loops the binoculars around her neck and tucks them under her t-shirt. "Get in the water and take a few deep breaths. The passage that leads out of the pool is about six feet down. I'll lead the way. Don't worry, it's not far."

Your hand trembles a little even though you're a pretty good swimmer. This is a new experience. Hopefully Wanda knows what she's doing.

You follow Wanda's light as she dives. At least she isn't lying about it not being far to the other side.

When you resurface, you're in a long narrow cave. The

cave's mouth is a circle of light shining in the distance. The ocean swell pushes into it from the open sea beyond.

"You scared?" Wanda asks as she treads water.

"A little," you say, rising slightly on an incoming wave.

"Well, don't worry," says Wanda. "I swim like a fish. Just follow me and you'll be fine."

The two of you swim towards the sunlight and out into a small bay. Birds circle overhead. Once at the beach, it's a short clamber over the rocks to the foot of a ladder. "Looks a long way up."

"Easy peasy. I've climbed it hundreds of times."

"Hundreds?" you ask.

Wanda smiles and shrugs. "Well, tens of times."

It's not as if you have much of a choice now. You've come this far.

"Righty ho, up we go." She wedges the flashlight into a crack in the cliff, grabs a rung and hauls herself up the ladder.

You follow.

Water drips like rain from Wanda's wet clothing and alarmed seabirds screech from their nests in the cliff, distracting you as you climb. A few daring birds divebomb you, swooping fearlessly near your head. Thankfully, they're more squawk than peck and you arrive at the top with both eyes intact.

"Crazy birds! That last one nearly got me."

"You must look like a hungry predator," Wanda says with a grin. "They're very protective of their chicks, you know."

"Yeah, right," you grin back. "Like sea-bird sandwiches are my favorite food."

"What, you don't like fishy chicken?" Wanda says, eyes laughing.

"No. I prefer nuggets."

"Well, if we're not going to catch a seagull for dinner, we'd better go and see what those men are doing."

Further along the cliff is a spot where a couple of leafy trees cling to the rocks. From there you can see most of the lagoon and across the treetops to the dome.

On the beach, by two palm trees, sits one of the men minding the inflatable.

"The other two must have gone inland," you say.

"Find a spot in the shade. With any luck they'll think the island is deserted and leave again."

You shake your head. "If they've come this far, they're sure to stay the night at least. It'll give them a chance to have a good night's sleep. No watches to do. No waves to worry about. They must be exhausted from fighting the storm. Believe me, I know."

"You're the sailor," Wanda concedes.

For a while, nothing happens. Then you spot movement. "There they are," you whisper, pointing towards the edge of the jungle. "On the path by the palms."

Wanda raises the binoculars.

The man on the beach hears his friends coming and stands up.

"Oh no, they've got a cat," Wanda whimpers.

The men move onto the beach, struggling with a bundle of fur entangled in netting. They maneuver the cat into the inflatable, drag the boat into the water and climb aboard.

Wanda looks at you. Beads of sweat glisten on her forehead and she's gone pale. "We have a big problem."

"Why?"

"If they get that cat back to the mainland, the media will go nuts. We'll never have a moment's peace, and my parents' chance to study the cats in their natural habitat will be ruined. We might even have to move back to Sydney."

A tear trickles down her face.

"Well, let's do something then," you say, jumping to your feet.

"But what? There are three of them, and my parents aren't due back for days."

It's time to come up with a solution. What do you suggest to Wanda?

Do you suggest that you:

Wait until nightfall, sneak on to the yacht and free the cat? **P59**

Or:

Go to the yacht and demand the cat's release? **P66**

Run and leap over the cats to escape

You've got to get out of here. Missing crewmembers, hungry cats and a weird woman. It's all too risky. If you don't move now, you may not have a chance.

You crouch ever so slightly, then spring forward, take two strides, and hurdle the cats blocking the doorway.

Whew! You've caught them by surprise.

But rather than taking the path back the way you came, you jink to the left around the back of the shack. The plan is to work your way through the jungle back down to the lagoon.

You're about to barge into the jungle when you see a pile of bones.

They look fresh. On top of the bones is the EPIRB from *Wanderlust.*

You swoop down and snatch the strap of the emergency beacon as you run past.

Is that all that's left of your crew? Have the cats devoured them? You fiddle with the EPIRB. A bright strobe flashes. Great. It's working.

Meow! Meow!

The cats are coming!

You tuck the EPIRB under one arm like a football and run in a blind panic, branches whipping your face as you plow headlong down the slope. The ground gets steeper. Before long you're sprinting so fast, you're not sure you could stop even if you wanted to.

With your right arm up in front of your face, you dodge left then right, avoiding trees. Your forearm takes a battering, but that's better than losing an eye, or damaging the EPIRB.

You don't stop to see if you're being chased. You don't stop to listen. You don't stop at all. It's not until you burst out of the jungle onto the pristine sand of the beach that you chance a look back.

For a moment, you turn around, cup a hand around your ear, and listen.

There's no rustling and no sign of the cats. But then cats are expert stalkers. For all you know there could be twenty of them looking at you right now. The thought sends a chill down your back despite the heat of the day.

After catching your breath, you jog down the beach. To where, exactly, you're not quite sure. But the further away from those cats and the old lady the better.

Halfway down the beach, out of the corner of your eye, you spot a tiny flash of orange in the jungle.

You skid to a stop and barge your way through the greenery towards it.

It's the life raft. Someone has thrown a few palm fronds over it to conceal it. Lucky you even spotted it.

"Ahoy?" you yell. "Anyone here?" Maybe the cats didn't get all your crew. Maybe those bones are from some other unfortunate group that landed here. You sure hope so.

Now you just need to evade the cats until someone

picks up the EPIRB's signal.

Staying with the raft is too obvious. The cats are sure to find you if you stay here. You could go inland, but you'd rather be near the beach when help arrives. A rescue helicopter can't land in the jungle. You decide to walk parallel to the beach along the edge of the jungle. That way you can still see the beach, but keep hidden from view.

Once you've covered a couple of hundred yards, you find a large fern and burrow in underneath it. You pull some of the dead fronds up for extra camouflage and lie still, breathing slow and steady.

It's about an hour before you hear the *whump, whump, whump* of the helicopter and crawl out of your hidey-hole.

There it is, a black dot coming in low over the reef. You grab the EPIRB and run onto the sand, waving your free arm.

Down the beach, you spot a group of cats. They're looking for you, of that you have no doubt.

When the cats see you on the beach, they rush towards you.

But then, as the chopper speeds towards your location, the cats realize they're too far away to reach you in time and scatter into the jungle.

By the time the chopper lands on the beach and the Australian naval pilot waves you aboard, there isn't a cat in sight.

One of the chopper's crew straps you into a seat and puts a pair of headphones over your ears. The helicopter lifts into the air and makes a sweep over the lagoon before heading out to sea.

"Welcome aboard," the pilot says through the headset. "I'm glad we found you. Your EPIRB came on eight hours ago, but before we could get an exact location, it went off again. You're lucky. We're pretty low on fuel. We were about to head back to the ship when it pinged again. Where's the rest of your crew?"

You gather your thoughts and watch the island get smaller and smaller through the chopper's window.

"I'm not sure," you say. "I suspect the crazy cat lady's animals have eaten them."

"Crazy cat lady?" the pilot says. His voice carrying a hint of skepticism. "On that island?"

"Yeah," you say. "We need to organize a search party, notify the police. I saw bones."

After the helicopter arrives back at the ship, the medical officer checks you over and patches up your injured arm and the bump on your head. You tell your story again. Despite being unsure of your tale, the navy sends the chopper and rescue team back to the island to check out your claim.

Three hours later, the chopper's back.

You can't believe your eyes when the skipper and other two crew members of *Wanderlust* jump out of the helicopter. They're alive! But how?

You race up to them, all smiles and confusion. "Ahoy, ahoy!"

After having a medical examination, *Wanderlust's* skipper sits and tells you their story.

"It's simple, really. The yacht was damaged and taking on water. I gave the order to abandon ship, but as we launched the raft, I noticed you weren't on deck. I was about to go below to get you when we got smashed by a huge wave. The safety line snapped and the three of us ended up in the water. We all managed to scramble aboard the raft, but the wind blew us away from the yacht so fast we had no chance of getting back to you. I was sure you were a goner."

"But what about the EPIRB and life jackets? How did the old woman get those?"

"Old woman?" The skipper frowns. "I don't know anything about that."

"So you're in the raft," you say. "Then what happened?"

"We set off the EPIRB. But before long, it stopped working. Not sure why. When we reached the island, we pulled the raft up above the high tide mark, and left the life jackets and the EPIRB on the beach so potential rescuers would see them. Then we set off looking for fresh water. The supply on the raft was contaminated. By the time we got back to the raft, the life jackets and

EPIRB were gone."

"So you never saw a crazy cat lady?"

The skipper scrunches his brow and shakes his head. "No… I would have remembered that."

"What about swimming cats? Did you see any of those?"

"No," says the skipper. "Are you okay?"

"But your gear? If the island's deserted, who took your stuff?"

"Yeah, we figured someone on the island took our stuff, so we walked around the island to see if we could find them. We'd just arrived back at the lagoon when the chopper turned up."

"So you didn't see anyone? No old lady, no cats, nothing?"

The skipper shakes his head. "According to the navy, this island is uninhabited."

"But how can it be?"

The skipper shrugs. "The navy doesn't care. They've saved everyone off the *Wanderlust*, that's all that matters to them."

"Hmmm…" you mumble. "This is weird."

The skipper leans forward. "The navy did find some chimpanzee bones on the island. Seems there was a colony abandoned there after World War Two ended. But they swear people haven't lived on the island since the 1970s."

"But I saw—"

"Yeah, you told us. And because of the life jackets going missing, I tend to believe you. But what can I do about it? The navy has places to be, they can't spend time on wild cat chases."

"But…"

Then you realize that nobody cares. Why argue? You're just a kid with an unlikely story. The navy has more important things to worry about.

It's at that moment you decide you're going to come back to the island one day. Come back and prove that there are swimming cats. Maybe the old woman will still be here too. But for now, all you want is something to eat and a nice long sleep.

Congratulations, you've finished this part of the story. But have you met Wanda, the chimps or the octopus? There are many paths this story can take. What would happen if you start again and make different decisions?

It's time to choose. Do you:

Go back to the beginning and take a different path? **P127** Or

Go to the Big List of Choices and find parts of the story you've missed? **P125**

Wait until nightfall and sneak on to yacht

The men row the inflatable boat to the yacht. They spend some time getting the cat into a wire cage sitting on deck. There is much hissing from the cat and a yelp or two from the men.

"Let's wait until dark. Then we can sneak aboard and free the cat," you suggest.

Wanda studies your face as she thinks. "Hmmm. Maybe."

"Got a better idea?"

She shakes her head as more tears streak down her cheeks.

"Look, Wanda, these guys are exhausted from battling the storm…"

"And the cat."

"Yeah, and the cat. Once they're asleep, they won't hear a thing. We'll only be on the boat long enough to open the cage."

She wipes her eye and attempts a smile. "Okay. If you think it'll work."

Time seems to move slowly when you're waiting and today is no different. You and Wanda sneak back to a spot near the beach and wait in the bushes for your chance.

As the sun sinks, the shadows grow longer and a light offshore breeze comes up. Ripples on the calm sea outside the lagoon entrance reflect the last of the sun's rays and make the ocean dance with pink and silver.

The three men, flushed with their successful cat hunt, sit in the cockpit passing a bottle of rum around. As the level of liquor in the bottom lowers, their talking becomes louder and more animated. Once empty, the first bottle is tossed over the side and another is fetched from below.

The moon rises above the horizon as the men finish the second bottle. By the time they head below to sleep, they are all staggering drunk.

You roll onto your side and whisper into Wanda's ear. "Let's give them a bit of time to make sure they're asleep. Then we'll get going."

"This is going to be easy," you say, half an hour later. "They were so drunk, we could do almost any—" Your mouth snaps shut as the idea hits you.

"Almost any what?"

"Come," you say, standing up. "I'll show you."

You take off your shoes and wade into the warm water of the lagoon.

Wanda follows as you dogpaddle out to the yacht.

At the back of the boat, you climb the boarding ladder and gently step down into the cockpit. A quick peek through the hatch into the cabin below shows the men sprawled out, sound asleep. The reek of alcohol is strong, and one of the men is snoring loudly.

You return to the stern and wave Wanda aboard.

"Go let the cat out," you whisper. "I'll get on with my plan."

While Wanda creeps forward to open the cage door, you scope out the controls in the cockpit. When you find the control for the anchor winch, you press the up button and hear the faint whine of the anchor rope winding onto the capstan. The yacht moves forward as the anchor rope is pulled tight, but you hit the stop button before the anchor lifts off the bottom.

When you look forward, Wanda seems to be struggling to open the cat cage.

As you move forward to help, you notice a dark shape slither over the deck. It's Oscar.

Tentacles reach for the twisted wire holding the cage door closed, and moments later the cat is winding around Wanda's legs.

"Thanks, Oscar," Wanda says as the octopus slithers back into the water.

You shake your head, not quite believing what you've just seen. "Go on, get back to the island with the cat. I'll take it from here."

"But what are you going to do?"

"You'll see."

Cuddling the cat, Wanda makes her way back to the boarding ladder and slips quietly into the water. "Be careful," she whispers.

You wave her away and then untie the rope holding

the mainsail on to the top of the boom. Next, you locate the rope that raises the mainsail and pull. It's heavy, but you haul away until it's up and secured.

As the sail flaps gently in the breeze, you rush back to the cockpit, grab the rope attached to the boom and wrap it around a big winch near the cockpit and crank the handle. As you wind in the rope, the boom swings around and the sail fills with wind.

Your thumb hits the up button on the anchor winch.

As soon as the anchor is off the bottom, the yacht begins to move.

You grab the tiller, point the bow of the yacht towards the lagoon entrance, and then tie it to the rail to hold it in position. As you do this, the sail billows out and the yacht increases speed.

A quick trim of the sail and before long the boat is gliding along at six knots, virtually sailing itself.

Just one last thing.

On the table, down below, you spotted a navigational chart and a handheld GPS unit. This will be how the men found the island in the first place.

You creep down the steps into the saloon, grab the GPS, slide the chart off the table, and make your way back up the steps. The GPS makes a splash as it hits the water of the lagoon. The map you fold up and tuck into the waistband of your shorts for safe keeping.

The yacht picks up speed.

One last check it's still on course and you climb over

the stern, down the ladder and slip into the sea.

As you dogpaddle back to shore, you watch the yacht sail through the gap in the lagoon and out to sea. It will be hours before the men wake up. By then they'll be over the horizon and miles away. Without a chart and their GPS. They'll have little chance of finding the island again any time soon.

When you reach the beach, Wanda and the cat are waiting for you.

Wanda smiles as the cat rubs against your leg. "I think she likes you."

As you bend down to give the rescued cat a scratch, another half-dozen cats wander out of the jungle onto the beach.

One by one, the cats enter the lagoon and disappear.

"Where are they going?" you ask.

"Night fishing. It's always good when the moon is up."

You stare at Wanda, wondering if she's just joking with you. But then you hear a splash out in the lagoon and turn to see cats leaping out of the water after a school of silver fish.

"Of course, night fishing. Why didn't I think of that?"

Later, Wanda leads you back to the tree house. "It's time for me to radio my parents. I'll let them know you're here and that your crew is missing."

"Right, my crew. With all the drama, I'd forgotten."

The radio is a big old thing with heaps of dials and a handset attached to it with a long black cord. It sits on a wooden desk in a room off the kitchen. Wanda sits down, flips a few switches, and turns various knobs. She picks up the handset and pushes a button on its side. "Wanda to *Gerty*. Come in, *Gerty*."

Static crackles as Wanda fiddles with the dials.

She turns towards you and giggles. "Why don't you go and make us some seagull sandwiches while I do this? Sometimes it takes a while to get through."

Your stomach's been rumbling for a while now, so she doesn't have to ask twice. By the time you've spread peanut butter and jam on bread and eaten half of your sandwich, Wanda's joined you.

"You'll be pleased to know the crew of *Wanderlust* was picked up by a merchant ship early this morning about thirty miles north of the island. Everyone's safe."

"That's a relief."

"They also said they'll organize someone to come and pick you up as soon as possible."

"Any idea how long that will be?"

"There's a naval exercise going on nearby so Dad reckons they'll divert one of their choppers in the morning. He's also going to get them to look for those poachers on the yacht. With our statements, they should be able to charge them and impound their boat."

You smile. "So the cats will be safe?"

She nods. "Looks that way. For now, at least."

You take a bite of your sandwich.

Wanda smiles. "So how's that seagull tasting?"

Congratulations. This part of your story is over. You've successfully defended the aquatic cats and will soon be rescued. You reach down and feel the map folded up in your waistband, hidden under your t-shirt. It shows the location of the island. Maybe when you're old enough, you'll get a boat of your own and come back.

But for now, it's time for another decision. Have you read all the different paths the story can take? A good place to make sure you haven't missed anything important is to check out the Big List of Choices.

So what now? Do you:

Go back to the beginning of the story and take a different path? **P127**

Or

Go to the Big List of Choices? **P125**

Demand the release of the cat

That poor cat! You have to do something right now. "I'm going to swim out to that yacht and demand they release it."

Wanda's eyes narrow. "Is that smart? You don't know those men."

But you're not listening. You're on your way down the path towards the beach. When you get there, you take off your shoes and plunge into the lagoon.

Wanda reluctantly follows you to the beach, but doesn't enter the water. "Be careful," she says as you swim towards the yacht.

At the stern of the yacht, you climb up the boarding ladder.

Two of the men are on deck looking at the cat which they've locked into a cage on the deck.

"Hey, you! Give me my cat! I've alerted the authorities. Cats on this island are a protected species!" It's a weak bluff, but it's the only thing you can come up with at short notice.

The men turn and look up at you. "And who might you be?"

"Never mind who I am. Give me my cat!

While you're arguing with the men on deck, the leader of the group storms up from below, grabs you by the collar, and throws you over the side. Your head hits the side of the boat and everything goes black.

Glug,

glug,

glug.

I'm sorry, this part of your story is over. Unfortunately, these men are vicious criminals, interested only in the profit they can make from selling the aquatic cat to a collector. You shouldn't have taken them on by yourself without having a plan.

Lucky for you this is a You Say Which Way adventure and you can go back and make that last decision differently. Or you can go to the Big List of Choices and read from another part of the book. The Big List of Choices is also a good place to check that you haven't missed parts of the story.

So what now? Do you:

Go back and decide to wait for night and sneak onto the yacht? **P59**

Or

Go to the Big List of Choices? **P125**

Make an excuse

There is something not quite right with Wanda. You don't know exactly what, but your gut tells you not to trust her.

"I'd rather go back and look for the rest of the crew. They could be injured and need my help."

"Sure, if that's what you want," she says.

"Can you take me back to the surface?"

Wanda shrugs, then leads you back to the small white room by the elevator. "If you get hungry later on, just come back down and go to the laboratory. I've got a whole heap of homework to do before my parents get back."

After the elevator rises to the top of the dome, you have a quick look around and then head towards the lagoon. But before you get halfway there, you have this funny feeling that something or someone is following you.

You pick up your pace.

Around the next bend in the path, you duck in behind a big fern and crouch down, hoping to see if your hunch is right.

But it's not Wanda who's following you. It's a cat the size of a cheetah with paws bigger than your hands and a tail at least three feet long.

You hold your breath and slump even lower, hoping it doesn't see you. For a moment you think you've been successful in your attempt to hide, but as the huge cat is about to pass your position, it stops, snaps its head around and stares at you with bright yellow eyes.

Startled, the cat arches its back, its short hair standing on end.

"Nice kitty," you say, holding your hand up in front of your face for protection.

The cat's hair lies back down as it sees you mean it no harm. But it continues to stare.

"You're a big one, aren't you, kitty," you say, slowly standing to full height.

When the cat pounces, you're not expecting it. Its front paws hit you square in the chest and knock you off balance. Luckily, the ground is sandy and your landing isn't too hard. Now you're flat on your back and the big cat is sitting on your chest. Its breath smells of fish.

"Ni-nice kitty," you say, hoping it doesn't eat your face.

You take a big breath and are about to scream, when it leans in, licks your face, and starts purring.

Phew!

You reach up and give the cat a scratch behind the ears as it licks you again and again. "Good kitty. Now can you please let me up?"

"Kong! Get off."

It's Wanda.

The cat leaps off you and winds around Wanda's legs, nearly tripping her up.

"I'm glad you're here," you say, sitting up. "I thought he was going to lick me to death. His tongue is so rough!"

Wanda kneels down so that she's eye to eye with the big cat and gives him a scratch behind the ears. "Yeah, he can be overly friendly at times. You should see what he'll do for fish."

You stand up and brush the sand off your backside. "How'd he get so big?"

Wanda smiles. "That's what my parents are trying to find out. A mutant gene caused by a radiation leak is their latest theory. Problem is my parents can't find the source of any radiation."

As you're thinking about that, Wanda gives Kong one last scratch and stands up. "I thought I'd better come and help you look for your crew. This place can be dangerous if you don't know your way around."

"More dangerous than giant cats?"

"You bet," Wanda says as the cat runs off into the jungle. "Have you ever been attacked by coconut crabs? Or been between a chimpanzee mother and her baby?"

"Really? Chimps on this island?" you ask, wondering if Wanda is joking. "There aren't normally chimpanzees on islands in the Pacific."

"These chimps were brought here by the Americans after they liberated them from a Japanese lab during the war. When the Americans went home, they left the chimps behind."

"That's a bit mean."

"They've done okay," Wanda says. "But they're not fond of strangers, so I thought I'd better come along to help."

"Thanks," you say, pleased that she did. Maybe you've judged Wanda wrong. Maybe she's okay after all. "I just want to find my crew and go home."

Wanda smiles. "Well, we better get a move on then. Oh, and watch out for crabs. One or two you can outrun, but if you get cornered…"

There is no sign of the crew when you get to the beach, so the two of you head towards the rocky point to the north where there's a narrow track that leads up to a promontory overlooking the lagoon and, you suspect, much of the rest of the island.

"I'm… not even… sure they're on… the island," you say between gulps of air as you climb the steep track. "The life raft… could have… drifted anywhere."

At the top of the track, with hands on knees, you catch your breath before looking around.

"There they are," Wanda says, pointing towards an orange dot a couple of miles offshore.

You don't see the raft until you shield your eyes from the glaring sun. "Good spotting. But what now?"

Wanda thinks for a moment. "The wind is blowing them the wrong way. They can't paddle against that."

"So what do we do?"

"Time to get the catamaran."

"You've got one of those?"

A grin crosses her face. "Well, it's not your run-of-the-mill catamaran."

"Not run-of-the-mill? What do you mean?"

Sensing your confusion, she turns towards the track. "Probably easier if I show you."

Without waiting for a reply, Wanda scurries back down the path to the lagoon. On the edge of the jungle, she lifts up a couple of large palm fronds and exposes an outrigger canoe. The main hull seats two, and it has a smaller hull attached to the main hull with branches for stability.

"This is an outrigger canoe, not a catamaran," you say, a little confused. "If you think I'm going to paddle out to the life raft with this breeze blowing, you're crazy."

"Except, as I said, this isn't a typical catamaran. Now stop whining and help me get this into the water."

As you help Wanda drag the outrigger into the lagoon, you notice it has an unusual attachment on the back pole that runs between the small outrigger and the main hull of the canoe. You're about to ask her what it's for when she takes an oval piece of wood attached to a long cord and begins whirling it around in a circle over her head.

Vroom, vroom, vroom, vroom. Vroom, vroom, vroom, vroom, hums the contraption as it whips round and round in a circle.

After half a minute, she stops, wraps up the cord, puts

the thing back in her pocket and sits down on the warm sunbaked sand.

"What the heck was that thing?"

"A bullroarer," she says.

"So what now?"

"Now we wait."

Your brow creases. "Wait for what?"

"For our engine."

"Huh?" Now you really are confused. But rather than ask more questions, you sit beside her and wait, thinking all the while what possible type of engine you can conjure up by whizzing a bullroarer around your head.

Then you see the cats. There's half a dozen of them, not quite the size of Kong, but big enough.

"Our engine's arrived. Climb aboard."

You do as she asks.

Then Wanda grabs the only paddle and sits behind you.

The cats enter the water, grab the attachment on the pole between the two hulls with their front paws, and start swishing their tails back and forth in the water.

Before you know it, the outrigger canoe is moving along at a good speed.

"See, I told you it was a catamaran."

"But how the heck did you train them to do this?" you ask, astounded.

Wanda gives you a cheeky grin. "Bribery."

"Bribery?" you say.

"I bribe them with fish," Wanda replies. "When we get back from our jaunt, they'll each get a nice feed of fish."

"And that's all it takes?"

"It takes a little training, but cats are simple creatures. Sleep and fish. Get those two components in balance and they'll do pretty much whatever you ask."

As the catamaran cruises through the gap in the reef, Wanda makes an adjustment to your course with the paddle. The craft handles the slight chop caused by the wind without a problem, and the cats seem tireless in their tail swishing.

In half an hour or so, you can see faces in the life raft. Confused faces, but smiley ones nonetheless.

"Ahoy!" you yell. "Looks like you could use a tow!"

When it comes to being rescued, the crew isn't too worried that it's an outrigger powered by six unusually large cats doing the rescuing. They know there'll be plenty of time for questions once everyone's back on dry land.

"About time you showed up," the yacht's skipper says with a wink. "What kept ya?"

Wanda laughs and tosses the skipper a rope and turns the outrigger towards the shore.

On the trip back, Wanda and the crew on the life raft paddle to help out the cats. But even against the breeze, it only takes half an hour to reach the calm of the lagoon.

As the crew pulls the life raft up the beach, Wanda

grabs your arm. "I'd better go and feed these bad boys, otherwise they'll never help me again. I'll see you later."

You nod. "Thanks. Your catamaran is brilliant."

And with that, Wanda and her six helpers head off towards the dome.

"Who was that?' the yacht's skipper asks.

"Wanda. She and her parents live here."

The skipper looks confused. "That's weird. This island is meant to be deserted."

"Is it?" you ask.

"That's what the charts say."

You're about to ask the skipper another question when the ground starts vibrating. Not a shaking like an earthquake, more like a high-pitched hum.

"What the heck is that?" the skipper says.

Then you see what you thought was a stone dome slowly rising above the jungle. It's not a dome at all. It's a huge flying disk!

The disk flies towards your group on the beach and stops. Through a window on the side of the disk, you see Wanda and Kong.

Wanda waves once and the disk streaks off over the ocean towards the horizon.

"Hey, wake up. It's your watch!"

"What?" you say, dragging your head up off the pillow.

It's the skipper. "It's your watch. Get your wet weather gear on and get up on deck."

Wait? What? Has it all been a dream?

Outside, the storm is still raging and it looks like you have another wet and wild four hour watch to do.

It must have been a dream.

Beside you, a crewmate is putting on her gear to go topside. "Wait till I tell you the crazy dream I had!' she says.

You fasten your jacket and look over at her. "Were there swimming cats?"

Her mouth drops open. "How the heck did you know that?"

Congratulations, this part of your story is over. But have you read all the other possible paths the story can take? You might even want to go to the Big List of Choices to find parts of the story you've missed.

It is time to make a decision. Do you:

Go back to the beginning of the story and make different decisions? **P127**

Or

Go to the Big List of Choices and find story you've missed? **P125**

Let go of the cats and climb up the ladder

You've never been a big fan of caves, so you let go of the cats and swim over to the ladder. It's high tide, so the bottom rung is under water.

The ladder is rusty, but it holds your weight, no problem. As long as the thing doesn't pull away from the rock wall, you should be fine.

But it's a long way up, and the seagulls nesting on the cliff aren't very welcoming. They must think you're trying to harm their chicks.

By the time you're halfway up the ladder, the gulls are divebombing you in teams of two or three at a time. When one pecks you on the back of the head, you nearly fall.

You climb and dodge birds with equal effort. When you finally reach the top, sweat is running down your forehead in rivers and your hands are covered in rusty brown flakes.

You collapse on the ground, close your eyes, and breathe deeply.

"Dem birds is crazy," a voice says.

You sit up and turn towards the sound. It's an old woman with silver-grey hair tied in a bun, wearing a white apron over a faded blue dress. Her face is brown and wrinkled from the sun, but her eyes and teeth sparkle. Weaving around her ankles are half a dozen cats.

"They sure are," you reply.

"Lucky ya didn't fall off wid dem birds a pecking at ya like dat."

You get to your knees and then stand up. The cats gathered around her are similar to the ones in the water. Long tails. Bigger than average paws. "These are like the cats that saved me."

"Dey's good cats," the woman says. "Good hunters." She bends down and gives one of the cats a scratch. "Good kitties."

With that, the old woman turns and walks along a path that leads down a steep ridge towards the lagoon.

Her cats follow.

"Comin'?" she shouts over her shoulder.

It's not as if you have anywhere else to go, so you leap up and fall in line.

About halfway down the ridge track, the woman veers off into a glade of palms. The umbrella of leaves blocks the harsh sun and causes an instant drop in temperature.

"My place is just down here," the woman says, pointing. "Come and meet the family."

When you enter her weather-beaten shack, you discover her family is another twenty or so cats. They all look alike. Grey. Short hair. Long tails. Big paws. Smelly.

"Ain't dey beautiful?" the woman asks with a smile. "Best cats in the world."

"Ummm… Yeah… Beautiful." But by now, your eyes are watering from the stench of cat pee. "I don't suppose you've got a phone or a radio I could borrow. I need to report that our yacht sunk and try to find my crew."

"Oh no. We ain't got no radio."

It's then you see three life jackets from the *Wanderlust* sitting in the corner. You point and say, "Where'd you get those?"

"Found 'em washed up on the beach dis morning."

"Did you see any of my crew?"

She shakes her head and looks down at the ground. Why won't she look you in the eye? Is she lying? Has she done something to the crew?

"Look, I think I'd better get going and see if I can find my friends." You move towards the door.

Meow!

Three big cats block the doorway.

"But the cats want you to stay," the woman says, rubbing her withered hands together. "Don't you like my babies? They really like you, don't y'all?"

You look around. All the cats are staring at you. A couple lick their lips.

You try to move past the cats blocking the door, but a swipe from an over-sized paw sends you jumping back. "Ouch!"

"I said, dey want you to stay!"

This is crazy. What do you do? Do you:

Run and leap over the cats to escape? **P52**

Or

Stay and try to talk your way out of this mess? **P91**

Go to the laboratory

As the door to the lab swings open, your eyes widen. "What the heck?"

A row of large glass tubes hangs suspended from the ceiling. Red liquid drips into the top of each container from a tangle of rubber hoses that snake across the ceiling, down the wall and into various stainless-steel vats. A shiver runs down your spine when you realize that a chimpanzee floats motionless in each of the jars.

In the nearest tube, the chimpanzee's eyes pop open. It stares at you for a moment, then closes them again.

You move around the laboratory, inspecting the strange sight. Most of the chimps are sound asleep, unaware of your presence. It's gone cold, so you wrap your arms around your torso and hug yourself for warmth. This place is so weird—like a scene from a science fiction movie.

Why is somebody keeping chimps in these huge test tubes?

When the door clunks behind you, you nearly jump out of your skin.

It's a girl about your age wearing a t-shirt and shorts. "Where did you come from?" she asks with a scowl. "And what makes you think you're allowed in my parents' lab?"

"Sorry," you reply. "I'm looking for my friends. We sank—I mean our boat sank."

The girl tilts her head and gives you the once-over. You can tell she's trying to figure out if you're telling the truth.

"I swam to shore and then climbed up the dome hoping to spot them."

Her head nods a little as she takes in this information. "How did you get separated?"

"We got hit by the storm. I finished my watch and crashed out in my bunk. When I woke up, the crew was gone. The yacht was sinking, so I had to abandon ship."

"They left you behind?"

You nod and feel your face redden. "I had to swim for it. The life raft was missing... but I don't think they abandoned me intentionally," you say, trying to convince yourself as much as anyone.

Her eyes narrow. She seems unsure of your story, but at least her scowl is gone. "Hmmm..."

"Where are your parents? Maybe they can help me find them."

She hesitates a moment and rubs her bottom lip with a finger. "They're on a supply run. Be back in a couple of days."

"So no help from them then," you say, feeling disappointed but also wondering if she's telling you the truth. "What is this place?"

"It used to be a secret military base. My parents decided it would be an ideal place to set up their experiments."

You nod towards one of the glass chambers. "And the chimps? Don't they drown in that liquid?"

She shakes her head. "My parents are developing a sleep gel that can be used for space travel."

"Space travel?"

"The chimps get their oxygen and other nutrients from the gel. The theory is that by adding different chemicals to the gel, they can lower their heart rate and respiration down to a point where they can live in the gel for years and years without aging much."

"Wow."

The corners of her mouth twitch in the smallest of smiles. "Eventually they'll try it out on people. Maybe one day we'll be able to travel between the stars."

"How do the chimps feel about it?" you ask.

"They weren't doing very well when my parents arrived on the island. Food was scarce. Some of them learned to open and eat coconuts, others managed to catch the giant coconut crabs that live on the island. But it was a hard life."

"Did you say giant coconut crabs?"

"Don't worry; you can outrun them if you keep in shape. Just don't fall asleep on the beach." She displays a row of perfectly white teeth. "Anyway, my parents gave the chimps food, nursed a few back to health, and over time the animals learned to trust them."

"And then your parents thought it was okay to experiment on them?"

"I know what you're thinking. Experimenting on them sounds cruel, but my parents don't harm the chimps. They like the gel."

"Really?"

"Dad says it's like a vacation for them. The chimps float around and sleep in the tanks for a few days, then when they come out, they get heaps of treats. Nowadays, they line up to be first into the tanks."

You can't imagine how breathing gel could be relaxing, but then who knows what chemicals are in it. "If you say so."

"My dad says he's going into the gel himself soon, now that he thinks they've got the mix right."

"Better him than me." You walk around, looking at the chimps. Despite your concern, they seem fine. Little bubbles rise from their noses as they slowly breathe in and out. "But this is a Pacific island. How did chimps get here?"

"There were eight chimps rescued from a Japanese research facility near the end of World War Two. The Americans kept them here while the base was operational. But once the base closed, the chimpanzees were set free to fend for themselves. Over the years, their numbers grew. But as their numbers grew, food became scarcer."

You rub the back of your head where you bumped it during the storm on the yacht. "How many chimps are on the island now?"

She smiles. "About twenty. Eight males, seven females. The rest are juveniles and babies. Did you know chimps can live to be over fifty, and the females only have a baby every five years or so?"

After a ten-minute lecture, you know more about chimps than you thought possible.

Your stomach rumbles. You haven't had anything to eat since yesterday evening, and that was only a protein bar. "Hey, I don't suppose you've got food in this place, I missed breakfast."

The girl walks over to a small fridge and pulls out a container of bananas. She tosses one to you. "Eat this. It should hold you over for a while."

You were really hoping for something like a sandwich. Maybe if you ask nicely…

It is time to make a decision. Do you:

Eat the banana? **P108**

Or

Ask nicely for a sandwich? **P99**

Wait with Wanda for the cats to find the crew

Less than an hour later, Kong is back. "Meow."

You turn to Wanda. "Have the cats found the crew?"

Wanda looks over at you and shrugs. "How should I know?"

"Bu–but you said the cats would find them. And Kong's back. Doesn't that mean…?"

"Mean what?"

"Tha–that…"

"All it means is that Kong wants fish."

"So what do we do?"

Kong stares at Wanda. "Meow!"

Wanda stands up on the capstone of the dome. "It means I'd better get him some. Wait here. I'll be right back."

You step off the capstone. Kong weaves around your ankles.

"Lift down," says Wanda.

As the capstone sinks, another stone slides over to cover the hole. It's as if the lift never existed.

"Just you and me now, eh, Kong?"

"MEOW!"

"Hurry up, Wanda," you mumble.

Kong sits and looks up at you. Then he leans forward and stretches his front legs, his rump rising, tail flicking back and forth. Pale white claws spring from Kong's oversized paws and scrape on the stone, leaving visible marks.

You feel a faint vibration beneath your feet, and with a whoosh, Wanda is back, with a woven bag that smells of fish.

Kong pads over to the bag and rubs his face against it. A loud purr rumbles to life.

"Crikey, Kong, give me a chance."

Wanda drops two fish on the ground. Kong wastes no time chomping into them. A minute later, he wants more.

Wanda squats down and stares at Kong eye to eye. "Did you find the people, Kong?"

Kong licks his lips and rubs up against Wanda's knee. Then he makes a series of short mews.

"That's his 'I've got something to show you' sound," Wanda says.

"Meow!"

Wanda empties the bag onto the ground. "All right, Kong, two more, then you've got to lead us to the people."

Kong tilts his head to the side, licks his lips and nods.

These fish are eaten as quickly as the first lot. Kong meows for more, but Wanda shakes her head and shows him the empty bag.

"You can have more fish after you take us to the people, Kong. Not before." Wanda looks over at you. "Come on, let's get going."

You follow as she sidles down the dome towards the

jungle.

Kong scampers past Wanda, and turns down a narrow path heading in the opposite direction as the lagoon.

Kong disappears into the dense shrubbery; you have only his tail to follow. Sleek and grey, it resembles a shark cutting through the water.

You and Wanda have to jog to keep up.

"Where's he taking us?" you ask.

"Towards the estuary, I think."

Wanda's right. Before long, you come to a small creek that winds its way through a mudflat exposed by the dropping tide. Seabirds poke their bills into the ooze searching for small crabs, worms and snails to eat. Crabs scuttle about in their endless hunt for scraps while bubbles appear where shellfish are buried just below the surface.

"Careful where you walk. There's quicksand near the stream sometimes. It really sucks to get caught in that."

"Ha! Sucks. I see what you did there, Wanda."

She shoots you a sneaky glance and giggles.

Kong leads you over a small sand dune and onto the beach. Then you see them, about a hundred yards away, sitting in the shade of a palm tree beside a deflated lift raft. The crew huddles together, bedraggled and scared, surrounded by at least fifty cats.

Wanda grins and pumps the air with her fist. "See! I told you Kong and his pride would come through!"

You cup your hands around your mouth and yell.

"Hey, Skipper! Looks like you've had a cat-tastrophy!"

Wanda rolls her eyes.

When the skipper sees you and Wanda heading his way, the relief on his face is obvious. "Can you get these critters to leave us alone?" he asks. "Every time we try to go to the creek to get some water, they hiss and scratch us. They've held us captive for nearly an hour. Look what they've done to the lift raft."

"Sure," you say.

As you, Wanda and Kong wade into the clowder of cats, they part down the middle. Wanda kneels down and says a few words into Kong's ear. At least three of which are 'fish'.

Wanda stands and smiles. "That should do it."

Kong makes mewing sounds and the other cats follow him to a shady spot ten yards away.

"Who's your friend?" the skipper asks. "Are these her cats?"

"This is Wanda. She and her parents live here."

The crew smile and say hi to Wanda.

Wanda looks over at the carpet of cats. "I promised my friends fish if they found you. I'd better go and feed them, otherwise they'll never help me again."

The skipper half-closes one eye and peers at Wanda suspiciously. "Help you... Right... Ummm, okay."

Wanda smiles. "Would you like me to radio my parents and get them to send someone to pick you up?"

The skipper shakes his head. "No need. We got

through to an Australian naval vessel on our emergency radio. They've dispatched a helicopter that will home in on our EPIRB nearly an hour ago. Should be here any time."

Wanda nods and then turns to you. "Well, it's been fun. Come again sometime. I'll show you around a bit more."

"Thanks," you reply. "I might just do that."

Wanda turns and heads back the way you came. Kong walks behind her, a string of cats in his wake. Just before she disappears behind the dune, she turns and waves goodbye one last time.

"Boy oh boy, them were some big ol' cats," the skipper says.

As you're about to agree, you hear the *whump, whump, whump* of a helicopter in the distance.

The skipper points towards a black dot skimming low over the reef. "Looks like our ride's arrived."

Pity it's come so soon. You would have liked to spend more time on the island. Get to know the cats, perhaps, or see what other surprises you might have found.

Lucky for you, this is a You Say Which Way adventure and you can go back and read a different path.

Don't you wonder what would have happened if you'd made different choices?

Congratulations, this part of your story is over. You survived and were rescued. But what do you want to do now? Do you:

Go back to the beginning and read a different path? **P127**

Or

Go to the Big List of Choices and find story lines you might have missed? **P125**

Stay and talk your way out of the mess

"I need to look for my crew," you say, trying to reason with the woman. "They could be injured and need my help."

The woman shakes her head. "Nah, dey don't need no help, do dey, kitties?"

"What do you mean, they don't need help? Have you seen them?"

"Sure, I seen dem. Kitties hungry. Dey don't need no help."

The cats move closer. A few have their claws out, ready to attack.

"Babies, dey hungry."

When the cats pounce, you don't stand a chance.

I'm sorry, but this part of your story is over. The mad cat lady has lured you back to her shack so her many cats have something to eat. But don't worry, if you like, you can go back and choose differently. What would have happened if you'd made a break for it?

It's time to make a decision. Do you:

Go back and make a run for it? **P52**

Or

Go back to the beginning? **P1**

Or

Go to the Big List of Choices? **P125**

Go look for the crew yourself

"Well, you may have faith in the cats, Wanda, but I think I'll go and do a bit of looking for myself."

Wanda raises her eyebrows and tilts her head. "Suit yourself. Just don't get lost. I've only got so much fish for bribes."

You stand up and look around. There's a trail leading away from the dome that looks like it heads to the far end of the lagoon. If the life raft managed to make it to the island, that would be a good place to come ashore.

"Bye, Wanda. I'll see you later."

Wanda scowls up at you. "Yeah, yeah. Off you go then." She jumps up and stands on the capstone of the dome with her back turned toward you. "Lift down!"

A moment later, she's gone.

"No need to storm off in a huff," you mumble as you head down the dome towards the path. "Pardon me if I don't think you can talk to cats."

But as you walk through the jungle, you wonder if you've made a mistake not waiting with Wanda. Even if she can't communicate with cats, you may need her help. Now that she's mad at you, she may be less willing to help in future.

The path leads through the jungle to a beach of golden sand. Standing by the water's edge, you look both ways for signs of the crew. The tide is high, so any footprints there might have been washed away.

The beach stretches for at least a mile before it curves around to the right and disappears out of sight. You decide to head that way and check it out.

Around the corner, the landscape changes dramatically. This is the rugged, exposed end of the island. Gone is the golden sand. Here, a jumble of rocks forms a barrier to the endless ocean rollers that crash ashore sending towers of white spray shooting skyward. What few palm trees exist on this part of the coast are twisted and lean at weird angles from the constant battering of storms.

If your crew came ashore along here, they'd be in trouble.

You scramble up a large boulder to get a better view of the surrounding area. No crew. No cats. Nothing. As you're about to scramble down again, you spot a weird-looking bird hovering off to your right. You put your hand to your forehead to shade your eyes from the glaring sunlight. Is it a bird? How can it be, it's just hovering there, not flying like a normal—

It's a drone!

You climb down from the rock and weave your way towards the drone.

You lift an arm, point up at the drone, and yell. "What's going on? Is that you, Wanda?"

The drone jinks a little left and then moves closer. It's a lot bigger than you first thought and looks military. It's about the size of a small car. Eight rotors whirr as it closes in. A long tube on the bottom swivels around and points towards you.

If that's a missile, you're in deep trouble.

The drone fires.

Not a missile, a net. A fine filament wraps around you before you have a chance to move. The more you wriggle to try to get it off, the more tangled you become.

When your feet get snagged, you fall to the ground.

"Hey! What do you think you're doing! Let me go!"

Now the drone is hovering closer. It winds in the cable attached to the net, and the net tightens around you like a drawstring bag. Then the drone rises, lifting you and the tangle of net into the air.

Once off the ground, rather than fighting to get out of the net, you're gripping it for grim death in case you fall.

The drone gains a little more altitude and then turns back over the jungle.

"Where are you taking me? Hey! Can anyone hear me?"

After flying for a minute or so, you relax. The view from up here is spectacular. You're high enough to see the entire island. You spot a group of chimpanzees up in a tree eating fruit.

A little further on, a huge treehouse appears, with numerous rooms and a viewing platform, way up in the canopy. Maybe if the drone lets you go, you could go and explore it.

Then the dome appears.

There's no sign of Wanda.

The drone carries on past the dome and out over the clear waters of the lagoon. You see the hull of the yacht lying on the bottom in about thirty feet of water. Its ghostly shape a shimmering pale blue.

Then about a couple of miles further out to sea, a naval ship appears. It's flying the Australian flag.

As you're lowered onto the ship, a number of people rush forward to untangle the netting and secure the drone to some D-rings on the deck.

It's not until you're free that you see your crew standing by the rail, grinning at you.

"We thought we'd lost you," the yacht's skipper says, resting his hands on your shoulders. "Didn't you hear me tell the crew to abandon ship?"

"I don't think so," you say, rubbing the lump on your head. "I must have taken a knock."

As the vibrations beneath your feet increase, you feel the ship begin to get underway, its wake a foaming line of white, its bow lifting into the slight swell.

"We'd just launched the life raft when a huge wave snapped the safety line and swept us all into the water," says the skipper. "The way the wind was blowing, we couldn't get back to the yacht to get you."

You feel relieved. "So you didn't abandon me?"

"No! We were frantic, but there was nothing we could do. I'm so happy you're okay."

"So how did you get here?" you ask.

"Thankfully, the navy was on an exercise in the area and picked up the signal from our EPIRB. We were only in the life raft for a couple of hours."

"So you never made it to the island?"

The skipper shakes his head "The navy tells me the island's deserted. We talked the captain into searching the island with their drone in case you'd made it ashore. What a stroke of luck they found you."

"But what about Wanda and the cats?" you say.

The skipper squints as he looks at you. "Wanda? Cats? Are you okay?"

You rub your head again. "Yeah, I–I think so."

He turns to one of the navy guys. "Hey! The kid's had a knock to the head and sounds a little delirious. We need to see the doctor."

"Bu–but I'm not delirious. There was a girl who has a pet octopus, and there's a huge treehouse and chimpanzees and swimming cats!"

You can tell by the look on your skipper's face he doesn't believe you.

"But I saw them!"

"Okay. Just take it easy," your skipper says as he leads you inside the ship. "Let's get the doctor to give you a quick checkup. Once he's done that, you can tell me all about it."

But you can tell he's just spinning you a line. You're just a kid. Why would they believe you?

Before stepping through the doorway, you turn to have one last look back at the island as it disappears over the horizon.

You have reached the end of this part of the story. You survived and have been rescued by the Australian navy. All your crew is safe too. Maybe once the doctor has given you the all clear they'll believe your story about the island, or maybe not.

As the doctor asks questions, shines a light into your eyes and pokes and prods you, you start making plans to get back to the island one day. If for no other reason than to let Wanda know you found your crew and are A-okay.

It is now time to make another decision. Do you:

Go back to the beginning of the book and read a different path? **P1**

Or

Go to the Big List of Choices and read from another part of the story? **P125**

Climb up the cliff and look for the crew

You look for a place to begin your climb. Off to the left a few yards is a narrow crack in the rock. That might give you some handholds on the way up.

At first, the climbing isn't too tough. But as you get higher, the hand and foot holds become fewer and fewer. As you near the top, you're forced to use the spindly shrubs growing on the cliff as handholds to pull yourself up.

It's a pity that these shrubs aren't very deeply rooted. As you grab one, it gives way and you fall.

I'm sorry, this part of your story is over. Unfortunately, the plant you grabbed onto couldn't hold your weight and caused you to fall thirty feet onto the rocks and hit your head. Now you're dead. Ooops!

Lucky for you this is a You Say Which Way adventure and you can go back and make that last decision differently. Or you can go back to the beginning of the story and start over. You can also go to the Big List of Choices and find other threads of the story to read.

So, what do you do? Do you:

Go back, make that last decision differently? **P22**
Or
Go back to the beginning? **P127**
Or
Go to the Big List of Choices? **P125**

Ask for a sandwich

"I'd rather have a peanut butter and jelly sandwich," you say. "Is that possible?"

"Sure," the girl says. "But before I take you home, I should probably know your name."

Having been the only kid on the yacht for the last two weeks, the crew gave you a nickname. It's not the most flattering of names, but you've become used to it. "The crew call me Shrimp."

The girl's eyebrows knit together. You and she are the same height. "Shrimp. Hmmm… My name's Wanda."

"Does that mean we can Wanda over to your place and get some food?" you ask with a grin, pleased with your pun.

She scowls at you. "Did you know that octopi eat shrimp?"

"They do?"

"And did you know I have a pet octopus?"

Is Wanda threatening you over a joke? "Sorry, I didn't mean…"

Her fists clench and she takes a step towards you.

You are about to turn and run when Wanda snorts.

"You should see the look on your face! I'm joking, silly!"

Phew. "So you don't have an octopus?"

"Oh, I have an octopus, all right. But Oscar prefers real shrimp."

"Lucky for me then. You had me worried."

Wanda's eyes laugh. Her eyebrows dance. "So, Shrimp, shall we go and grab that sandwich?"

Wanda leads you out of the lab, up the lift, down the stone face of the dome and along a path that heads towards the far side of the island. On this part of the island the jungle is dense, with taller trees and birds everywhere. The path tracks gently uphill, and once in a while you catch a glimpse of the ocean through gaps in the trees.

You hope it's not too far; it's been a long morning. "Where are we heading?"

"Our house is near the top of the island. It's not far now."

Wanda picks up the pace.

The two of you are making good progress when, without warning, your feet fly out from under you and you hit the ground with a *thwack!*

You've tripped. Or at least that's what you think until you feel a rumbling deep in the earth and the ground bucks beneath you.

"Earthquake!" Wanda shouts.

"Whoa!" You brace with arms and legs spread wide, your neck up to keep your head from bouncing in the dirt. You sneak a wobbling glance towards Wanda.

She's on the ground too, and not looking at all happy about it.

All around, trees sway like dancers, branches flailing. Shrubs shudder, leaves tremble. There is the thwack of coconuts hitting the ground—those things can kill you if they make a direct hit.

You try to stand, but only manage to get to your knees.

A minute later, all is silent. Even the birds have frozen in fear.

"Wow, that was a big one," Wanda says. "We need to get to high ground."

"High ground?"

"Tsunami. If it's long or strong, get gone. Haven't you heard that saying?"

You are about to ask Wanda more about the earthquake, but she cuts you off.

"Talk later. Let's go!"

She jogs off along the path without looking to see if you're following.

You saw a video of a big tsunami that hit Japan a few years back, so you know the damage they can do. You take off after her.

About five minutes later, around a slight bend in the path, you see a house perched high in the trees. It's like a fairytale house, with rooms, ladders and swing bridges built on different levels.

"You live in a treehouse?"

"Yes," Wanda says, glancing back over her shoulder. "Now hurry up and climb."

A ramp made of knotted vines and branches wraps around one of the tree trunks and spirals up to the house. More vines create a braided safety rail to keep you from falling.

It's about two stories up to the first room. You're breathing hard by the time you get there.

Your fingers sweep over the top of a large wooden table sitting in the middle of the room. "Wow, this place is awesome."

"Higher," Wander commands. "We've got to get higher."

She scurries up another ladder before wobbling across a narrow swing bridge to another tree about ten yards away.

You follow hesitantly. Once across the bridge, you discover a room with a set of bunk beds and a narrow set of steps that lead even higher.

Wanda keeps climbing.

"We call this the crow's nest," she says once you've both reached the top.

As you gaze out over the island, you spot the top of the dome in the distance. Beyond that, the bright blue water of the lagoon looks as tiny as a paddling pool. "Surely the tsunami can't get us way up here?"

Wanda shrugs. "Better safe than sorry. Now we wait."

Then you see the wave racing toward the island from the north. Your jaw drops. You raise a hand, point

towards the wall of water, and begin to speak. "Oh my—
"

"Looks like it'll hit the rocky side of the island," Wanda interrupts. "At least that should save the coral in the lagoon from too much damage."

The wave gets bigger as it approaches.

You turn to Wanda. "Look at the size of it!"

She gulps and grips the handrail. "You're not wrong."

From high in the crow's nest, you can tell the wave is a monster, and there's a dark line on the surface of the ocean that tells you another is close behind. Your rubbery knees are barely keeping you upright. Grabbing hold of a branch, you stare, transfixed, as the waves get closer.

"Crikey," Wanda mumbles, clutching your arm. "There's three of them."

When the first wave reaches the shallows, it piles up on itself and looms even higher before crashing violently onto the rocks. A cascading river of seawater rushes inland, picking up anything in its path. The chaotic mass rumbles like an approaching freight train. By the time the wave is two hundred yards inland, it carries sand, gravel, coconuts, branches, rocks and anything not fastened down. By the time the water is half a mile inland, it carries broken ferns, small trees and a tumble of other debris.

When the wave reaches the tree house, it has lost much of its momentum but the water is still six feet deep.

With a tortured screech, the ramp leading up to the house is ripped away from the trunk.

The crow's nest shudders as the water surges on.

Thirty seconds later, as if someone has flipped a switch, the water loses momentum, stops, then reverses course and begins its downhill race back to the sea, sucking everything, including the damaged ramp, along with it.

"Gebus! We dodged a bullet there," Wanda says.

The next wave hits less than a minute later. It's a little smaller and doesn't quite reach the tree house, but is still big enough to strip leaves off plants and scour the earth. The third wave is smaller again, but because most of the impediments to its progress have been cleared, it speeds inland, but then retreats just as fast.

When you look down into the jungle, you see a number of huge crabs clinging to the remaining trees and bushes.

"Coconut crabs?" you ask, pointing at a particularly large one on a nearby tree.

Wanda nods and then looks out over the canopy. "I hope the chimps are okay."

"I hope the rest of my crew is okay," you say, heading towards the ladder. "Let's go have a look."

Wanda shakes her head. "Wait. There might be more waves."

"More?"

"We have to wait at least an hour. Just to be sure.

Then if there aren't any more big shakes…"

Your stomach rumbles. "Plenty of time for a sandwich then. I'm starving."

Wanda leads you back down the ladder, across a swing bridge and into a room that doubles as a kitchen and dining room.

You lean over the railing and look below. "How are we going to get down? The ramp is missing."

Wanda surveys the damage, then turns and walks to a cupboard where she pulls out a tangle of cord and short planks. "We'll use this rope ladder. But first let's eat."

Just over an hour later, after a tasty lunch of peanut butter and jam sandwiches, Wanda ties one end of the rope ladder to a sturdy branch and throws the other end down to the ground. She grabs a bag of bananas from one of the cupboards and puts them into a coconut fibre bag which she loops over her shoulder.

"Hang on tight as you climb down," Wanda instructs. "This ladder can twist and throw you off if you're not careful."

A few minutes later, with nerves jangling, your foot touches the ground. Wanda is right behind you.

"So where to now?" you ask.

"Let's check the chimps first. My dad built them a shelter in a tree half a mile from here."

Without waiting, she tromps off into the jungle along a barely noticeable path. The jungle is already bouncing back from the beating. The ground is missing its normal collection of leaves and branches, and the odd tree is snapped off at its base, but considering the force of the water, you're surprised there isn't more damage.

Ten minutes later, a large tree appears just off the path to your right. Wanda stops and looks up. A platform of bamboo covered by a roof of palm fronds sits high in the fork of two branches. Upon it huddle the chimps.

A few of the juveniles bounce up and down, grunt and whoop. The adults are more wary.

"Come on, Hercules," Wanda calls out to a large male. "It's okay to come down now."

But Hercules is having none of it. He turns his head and looks away from Wanda.

It's not until Wanda pulls the bananas out of her bag and speaks to him in a singsong voice that Hercules is reassured and swings down to the ground.

The others soon follow.

"Crouch down and don't move," Wanda tells you. "Hercules is the leader of this community, and he'll want to check you out and make sure you're not a threat."

The large male is taller than you are when he stands on his hind legs. His frame is muscular. You've seen chimps on TV, but up close like this, they are more intimidating than you expected.

"Ooooh, ooooh," Hercules says softly as he picks at your clothes and sniffs. His wrinkled hand looks like a foot with fingers. He puts a finger under your jaw and lifts your face so that he can stare into your eyes.

His heavy brow is gray above deep-set reddish-brown eyes. It makes him look wise. His breath is warm, but not unpleasant.

"Friend, Hercules," Wanda says before turning to you. "Chimps use their sense of smell much more than humans."

"Ooooh, ooooh." Hercules grunts and has one last sniff before turning towards Wanda and taking a banana.

The rest of the chimps close in on Wanda's bag.

Wanda smiles. "Looks like you've passed the test."

"But what now?" you ask. "Do you think it's possible the rest of my crew has survived the tsunami?"

Wanda stands askew for a moment. One hand on her hip, the other under her chin.

"You're assuming they're even on the island," she says. "The wave hit the northern side of the island. If your friends are okay, they would have to be south of the dome, or on the cliffs overlooking the lagoon."

"We should go look for them," you say. "They could be injured."

Wanda nods. "Okay. You choose. Where do you want to go first?"

It is time to make a decision. Do you:

Look for the crew south of the dome? **P110**

Or

Go to the cliff overlooking the lagoon? **P113**

Eat the banana

You peel the banana and take a bite. It's a bit cool from being in the fridge, but your stomach is rumbling, and food is food. "Thanks," you say between bites.

The girl smiles. "My pleasure."

But by the time you've finished eating, you're feeling faint. Maybe it's all the stress you've been under the last few days.

As your knees begin to give way, the girl grabs your arms and helps you sit on the floor with your back against the wall.

Your eyelids are heavy.

"Just relax," the girl says. "Sleep."

When you wake up, you have a moment of panic, but it doesn't last. You breathe in more gel. Floating… Calm… Nice… You're in one of the tanks. But despite that, and having just woken up, you feel like nodding off again and getting back to that lovely dream you were having.

When you look through the glass of the big test tube, you see the girl with two older people standing quietly and observing you. The man makes notes on a tablet.

"Well done, Wanda," the woman says. "Now we just need to find the rest of the crew and our experiments can continue."

Maybe they will let you out of the tank one day. Or maybe not. In the meantime, that dream is calling.

I'm sorry to say that this part of your journey is over. You've been tricked into eating a drugged banana. Weren't you suspicious when she took it out of the fridge? You were in a secret medical lab filled with sleeping chimps. Eating food from strangers is never a good idea, especially in an unusual situation like that.

Lucky for you this is a You Say Which Way adventure and you can go back and make that last choice over again. Or you can go to the Big List of Choices and find another part of the story to read.

Do you:

Go back and ask nicely for a peanut butter and jelly sandwich? **P99**

Or

Go to the Big List of Choices? **P125**

Look for the crew south of the dome

"Time to head south then," Wanda says. "But don't get your hopes up."

These are not the words you want to hear. But Wanda's right. The waves were big. Half the island's been swept clean by them. If the crew's lucky, they'll be holed up somewhere south of the dome. If not... well, it doesn't bear thinking about.

You nod towards Wanda. "Let's do this."

Wanda doesn't waste any time. The trek south is like a forced march. "We need to get to the other side of the island quickly in case there's an aftershock. We don't want another wave to catch us."

You're about to ask Wanda if she always states the obvious, but you're puffing too much. Instead, you grit your teeth and try to keep up.

After skirting the dome, which hasn't been reached by the wave, Wanda slows the pace.

"Where do we look first?" you ask.

"Once we get back to the beach, we should follow the coast around the island."

"Okay," you say. "The life raft must have come ashore somewhere."

But walking around the coast isn't as easy as it sounds. Once you've left the sandy beach of the lagoon, the shoreline narrows and gets quite steep in places. Rocks poke through the sand and, in the distance, shapes the size of dinner plates litter the narrow beach.

Then you spot movement on the sand ahead. "Are those coconut crabs?"

"Yup. Just keep walking. There are only a few of them. We'll be fine."

Wanda lives here. She should know what she's doing... well, that's what you hope.

The first few crabs stand their ground, allowing the two of you to skirt them and carry on down the beach. But once you've passed a dozen or so, more come clambering out of the jungle. Before you get much further, more and more crabs pour out of the jungle. And all of them are heading your way.

"Crikey!" Wanda shouts. "I didn't think there'd be this many. Run!" She sprints down the beach.

In a flash, you're on her heels.

The two of you zigzag, dodging crabs, hurdling crabs, even kicking them out of your way. Pincers click and snap as you jink left, right, then left again. You increase the pace, pass Wanda, jink left, kick a crab and then leap over two more.

A hundred yards away the beach is empty, but in front of you is a carpet of crabs. Hundreds of them. Each with pincers held high, clicking and clacking—scuttling towards you.

You look towards the water. Is it safe? It looks deep.

The crabs are coming.

Click, clack, click.

Quick, it's time to make a decision. Do you:

Run into the water to escape the crabs? **P123**

Or

Keep running and hope to dodge the crabs before they get you? **P117**

Look for the crew on the cliff overlooking the lagoon

As you and Wanda walk through the jungle towards the cliff, things are getting back to normal. Birds sing. Butterflies flit. Midges buzz. Tree branches sway in the light breeze.

"We head up that path," Wanda says, pointing to a rocky path about two hundred yards away. "It follows a ridge to a lookout at the top. Just watch your footing."

About halfway to the top a parrot screeches from a grove of palms to your left.

"Is that a parrot?" you ask.

Without answering, Wanda takes off down a narrow track towards the sound.

"Wait for me!" you yell.

Wanda is fast. She ducks and dodges through the jungle with remarkable speed. It's not easy to keep up.

Within a minute, you've lost her.

You stop and listen.

Silence.

"Wanda!" you yell. "Wanda! Where are you?"

Nothing.

Wanda, where are you?

Is that a parrot?

"Is that you, Wanda?" you say.

Is that you, Wanda?

You push a branch aside and walk towards the echo. "Wanda? Can you hear me?"

Wanda, can you hear me?

Now the echo's above you.

You look up.

A brightly colored parrot sits on a branch. It looks down at you.

Hello. Polly wants a cracker, the parrot says.

"Where's Wanda?" you ask the parrot.

"How should I know, I'm a parrot."

You scratch you head. What's going on here?

Then Wanda appears from behind a tree. "How should I know, I'm a parrot," she says again in her parrot voice before cracking up with laughter. "Crikey, you're gullible."

You must admit, it's pretty funny. "Ha ha. You got me. Now can we get back to looking for my crew?"

"Polly wants a crew. Polly wants a crew. Squawk!" Wanda says before laughing again and retracing her steps back towards the cliff. "Follow me. Follow me. Squawk!"

By the time the two of you reach the lookout, the sky is a flaming orange. Clouds glow red and yellow. To the east, the ocean near the horizon is a deep blue.

Nowhere do you see the crew. At least this side of the island was untouched by the tsunami so if the crew are here, they should be safe.

It's not until you're heading back down the path that you see a spot of orange near the edge of the jungle beyond the lagoon about a mile away.

"Hey, I think I see the raft." You point. "There, way off in the distance. Do you see it?"

Wanda leans forward slightly and squints. "I think so. Hard to tell what it is from way up here. Better check it out. Better check it out. Squawk!"

You roll your eyes. "Give it a rest, Wanda. Let's go, it'll be dark soon."

Once back at the beach, you walk along the edge of the water where the sand is damp and the going a bit easier. You cross your fingers and hope the crew are okay as you make tracks to where you think you've seen the life raft.

As you get closer, the orange dot becomes more distinct. "It's the raft, all right," you say, picking up the pace.

But when you get to the raft, it's empty. At first, you think the crew must have drowned, but then you see a white piece of cloth tied to one of the oarlocks.

You rush over and untie it. "Look. A note."

Wanda moves closer as you unfold the piece of cloth. "What's it say?"

"It says they've been picked up by the Australian navy, and that they've left me the emergency locator beacon to use if I find the raft."

A funny look comes across Wanda's face. "So all you have to do to get rescued is set off the beacon?"

You nod. "Yeah."

"How long does the battery last?" Wanda kicks the

sand and looks at the ground.

"Oh heaps. Years, even."

"So you don't have to set it off right away?"

Then you get it. She hasn't had another kid to play with for ages.

"I could leave it a day or two, I suppose. When did you say your parents were getting back?"

A little grin crosses her face. "Another day or two, I reckon. Just enough time to give you a proper tour of the island."

You sling the EPIRB's strap over your shoulder and grin. "Sounds like a plan. I've always wanted to explore a tropical island."

A huge smile erupts across Wanda's face. "Cool. Follow me. Follow me. Squawk!"

Congratulation, you've reached the end of this part of the story. But have you tried all the different paths and made all the different decisions? Have you checked out the Big List of Choices to see what parts of the story you may have missed?

It's time to make another decision. Do you:

Go back to the beginning of the story and try a different path? **P1**

Or

Go to the Big List of Choices? **P125**

Keep running down the beach

"Don't go into the water!" Wanda screams. "There's way too many sharks on this side of the island."

"Now you tell me!" you say between ragged breaths.

Your foot lands on the back of one crab and then you leap to the back of another. It's like rock-hopping down a creek bed.

After the first few crab-hops, you get a rhythm going. But when you land on a particularly slimy crab, your foot slips and you go down in a tangle of legs.

Crab legs.

Lots of them.

A hard pinch nips your side.

Another nips your leg.

"Oww!" You struggle to your knees, but crabs are everywhere. With eyes closed, you swat crabs away from your face.

The crabs are winning the fight when an arm encircles your waist. You figure it must be Wanda's, but when you open your eyes, the arm is far too hairy and muscular.

Hercules tucks you by his side and does a bandy-legged sprint up the beach to the nearest tree. He tosses you up to the first branch and then swings up himself. He urges you higher before turning towards the jungle and emitting an ear-shattering series of howls.

His call is answered by the hoots and grunts of the chimpanzee troupe as they crash through the jungle towards your position.

The chimps stream past the tree and rush onto the beach where they grab a crab in each hand and crash them together like cymbal players in some strange orchestra before dropping them onto the sand and grabbing two more. As the crunching of crab shells and a cacophony of grunts and howls continue, Hercules drops to the ground and joins the fray.

Sensing danger, the remaining crabs scuttle off into the water, disappear into burrows, or retreat back into the jungle to hide amongst the dense shrubbery.

Victorious, the chimps sit in the sand and enjoy the spoils of the battle, a feast of crab cocktail au natural.

But where is Wanda?

You slither down from the tree and are about to go looking for her when you see a flash of color.

"Hey," Wanda says, stepping out of the jungle onto the beach. "Blimey, that was a close call."

"You're telling me," you say, pointing at the small cuts all over your legs. "Hercules saved me. I thought I was a goner."

"Coconut crabs don't stand a chance when the chimps are around."

Not far away, the chimps grunt, slurp, and crack open crab legs.

Wanda nods in their direction. "As you can see, they love crab meat. Wasn't much else for them to eat apart from coconuts and fish once the military departed."

Wanda bends down to pick up a leg that's become dislodged from one of the dead crabs. She cracks it in two and hands half of it to you. "Suck out the meat. It's yum."

She lifts the leg to her mouth and slurps loudly. Juice runs down her chin and a smile crosses her face. "Yum!"

"But it's raw," you say. "Shouldn't we cook it first?"

"Sorry," Wanda says, patting the pockets of her shorts. "I seem to have left my camp stove behind." She grins. "Believe me. It's fine. Just go for it."

Wanda's right. The crab meat is sweet and tender. As you eat, you spot a couple of cats wander out of the jungle. Big sleek ones with long tails.

Wanda sees them too. "They're after the scraps," she says between bites. "Amazing how they seem to know when the chimps have had a successful hunt."

You throw your eaten crab leg into the water. "We should get going. We're looking for my missing crew. Remember?"

Wanda smiles then tosses her empty crab leg over her shoulder. "Right. So we were."

Ten minutes later, about two hundred yards away, you spot a patch of orange near the edge of the jungle. "Hey, I think that's the life raft!"

You cross your fingers and break into a run.

"Ahoy!" you yell at the top of your voice. "Anyone there?"

"Shrimp?" A man's voice says. "Is that you?"

Then you see them. They're sitting in the shade of a big palm. The skipper leaps to his feet and rushes over to give you a big hug.

"Lucky you were on this side of the island," you say to the skipper. "Otherwise the tsunami might have got you."

"We thought we'd lost you too," the skipper says. "The storm was raging and we were taking on water. I told the other two to launch the life raft so we could abandon ship. I was just about to call you when a big wave knocked us all into the water."

"So you didn't leave me behind on purpose?"

The skipper's face drops. He looks hurt that you would think such a thing. "No, of course not. The life raft was inflating when the big wave hit, snapped the safety line and tossed us into the drink. We all managed to clamber aboard the raft, but the wind blew us away from the yacht so fast we didn't have a chance to get back to pick you up."

It all makes sense now. You should have known they wouldn't leave you behind.

You look up at the skipper. "So what now? How do we get home?"

"We sent an SOS on the emergency radio when we landed on the island. Our call was picked up by an Australian naval ship about two hundred miles south. It's launched a helicopter to come and pick us up. They'll home in on our EPIRB and should be here some time soon."

A wave of relief passes through you. You turn around to tell Wanda. But she's not behind you. "Wanda!" you yell.

The skipper scrunches his brow and peers at you. "Wanda? Who's Wanda?"

"A girl who lives here on the island," you reply. "She's been helping me. Her parents are scientists and they have a secret lab."

The skipper reaches out and lays his hand on your forehead. Does he think you're sick? Imagining things?

"She's real," you say. "She and the chimpanzees helped me fight off the huge coconut crabs after the tsunami!" You point at the nip marks on your legs. "See, crab bites."

You can tell that the crew is skeptical of your story. You are about to explain further when you hear the steady *whomp, whomp, whomp* of the helicopter.

The crew rushes to the water's edge and wave their arms above their heads.

You turn for a last look down the beach, hoping to catch a glimpse of Wanda, but there is no sign of her.

In a whirlwind of sand, the helicopter touches down. Its crew ushers you aboard, and before you've had a chance to think much about Wanda's disappearance, the helicopter is swooping over the lagoon before heading out to sea to rendezvous with its ship.

Sitting in the helicopter and looking back at the island as it slowly shrinks into the distance, you wonder if anyone will believe your story.

Maybe one day, when you're a bit older, you can come back on your own yacht and see how Wanda's getting on.

Congratulations, you've survived being shipwrecked on a mysterious island. You've made a friend, fought off giant crabs and lived through a tsunami. But have you followed all the different paths of this book? There are many different stories to read. The Big List of Choices is a good place to find parts of the story you may have missed.

It is time to make another decision. Do you:

Go back to the beginning of the story and try a different path? **P127**

Or

Go to the Big List of Choices? **P125**

Run into the water to escape the crabs

Crabs nip at your legs and feet as you hightail towards the ocean. After three splashing steps, you throw yourself forward and dive into the lukewarm water. After a few quick strokes, you spin around, tread water and stare back at the beach.

The saltwater stings your bleeding legs, but at least the crabs can't get you out here.

Wanda is bouncing around like some crazed dancer, avoiding crabs, when she spots your head protruding above the water.

She runs towards you and waves her arms, but stops before she's knee-deep in the water.

Her face has gone pale as she points frantically towards a grey shadow streaking towards you. "Shark!" she screams. "Get out of the water!"

But before you make it to shore, powerful jaws clamp onto your leg and drag you under. Yikes!

I'm sorry, but this part of your story is over. Unfortunately, you went into the water while you were bleeding and a hungry shark picked up your scent. Now you've become a shark's lunch.

Lucky for you this is a You Say Which Way story and you can go back and make that last decision differently. Or you can go to the Big List of Choices and find another part of the story to read.

Decision time. Do you:

Go back and decide to keep running down the beach? **P117**

Or

Go to the Big List of Choices? **P125**

Big List of Choices

Back at the beginning

As you know, the life raft is gone. Why would the rest of the crew leave without you? It makes no sense. They must have known you were asleep. Were you so tired you didn't hear the call to abandon ship? Have they gone to the island? But why use the life raft when the yacht is still floating?

Whatever the reason, you're here now. Alone. You'll just have to deal with it.

Maybe you should pump out the bilge. A yacht isn't much use if it fills with water. Or should you put out an emergency call on channel 16?

It's time for a decision. Do you:

Pump out the bilges? **P5**

Or

Put out an emergency call on the radio? **P8**

128

If you enjoyed this book, please leave a review on Amazon

Reviews help others know if this book is right for them. It only takes a moment.

Thanks from the You Say Which Way team.

More You Say Which Way Adventures

Secrets of Glass Mountain
Duel at Dawn
Volcano of Fire
Duel at Dawn
Missing Cat Mystery
Danger on Dolphin Island
Dragons Realm
Secret of the Singing Cave
Dinosaur Canyon
Deadline Delivery
Between The Stars
Pirate Island
Mystic Portal
Dungeon of Doom
Lost in Lion Country
Once Upon an Island
In the Magician's House
The Sorcerer's Maze Adventure Quiz
The Sorcerer's Maze Jungle Trek
The Sorcerer's Maze Time Machine

YouSayWhichWay.com

Printed in Great Britain
by Amazon